The Exit Interview

A Novel

M. Nariman

To Ryan and Ida.

Table of Contents

In Veritas Ex Memoria

David found himself lost. He was mad; how could *he* get lost? He had been on this trail many times before. But there was no use. What was done was done. Now, all he was thinking about was how to get back to his car, go home, shower, and go to bed.

He could not see the trail to the beach. He knew he was high up on the bluff. Heavy fog had obscured everything below. He checked his cell phone: no reception. Worse, the battery was running out.

Only a wedge-shaped structure could be seen on the property's vast grounds. David ran the length of the building to the cliff's edge; realizing the unexpected altitude, he ran back to the front. He was nervous now.

The lawn seemed to span a mile. A fountain was in the middle of the grounds. A road stretched from the entrance of the building, wrapped around the fountain, and disappeared in the distance.

The sun was setting. There were no other buildings nearby. He could only make out the silhouette of two lighthouses on the far corners of the bluff.

He sat on a bench next to the building and tried recollecting himself. What choices did he have? For a moment, he thought, maybe he should run to one of the lighthouses. He probably could not make it before dark. There was no guarantee that there would be any attendants anyway.

The building was enormous and didn't look like a house. "Could it be a secret security services bunker," he argued with himself, "even if it is, they can simply help me get back to my car." Then doubt set in, "What if they hold me and question me for hours?" He thought, "Too late. If they are from the government, they probably know I'm here already, and if anybody was concerned, they would have sent people to check me out by now." It seemed he had no choice but to ring the bell. He thought, "*What is the worst that can happen?*"

He walked around a bit, still puzzled. Then he went to the door: monolithic, no handle, no place to insert a key or a card. He was still looking for a doorbell when the door glided open. A woman greeted him; she was tall and slender with brown hair and green eyes. Her hair was short, cut too neat. Confident, authoritatively, "Amanda has been waiting for you. Please come in," she smiled vaguely.

David froze for a moment. Then he mumbled, "I don't think I know anybody called Amanda. I am just lost, em because of the fog." There was a loss of calm in his voice.

"That's okay—please come in," said the woman.

On the inside, the building looked like a house. Minimally decorated, vast, but at the same time warm. It did not seem to be a secret building of any type, which eased his anxiety.

First Contact

He was in awe of the vastness of the house. The majestic cathedral ceiling made him feel insignificant. There was a massive pipe organ right in the living room.

"I will be with you in just a few minutes. Please make yourself at home. I saw you coming up the trail. We have a camera, you know."

A woman was sitting on the bench before the organ's keyboard, facing away from him.

David answered, "I'm sorry. I didn't mean to trespass."

"No worries. I will be with you in a minute. I was practicing, and I appreciate a good audience."

Then, all he could hear was *Bach's Toccata and Fugue.*

There were no sofas or chairs. It felt awkward just to be standing in the foyer. David started walking towards the front of the living room. A single-piece curved glass in a thin silver frame constituted the window that stretched to the ceiling and across from one end of the room to the other. David seemed dazzled by the view and the whole setup. The light through the window seemed uniform as if all the highs and lows of the view were equalized. Just enough light was let through. He was pacing along the window up and down and enjoying Amanda's flawless performance.

As soon as the piece ended, she got up and came toward him. "I love music. It is amazing. Don't you think?" she extended her hand. She was jubilant. "My name is Amanda."

"I'm David. I apologize. It was too foggy out there. I couldn't find my way to the beach. My car is parked down there. I would not have intruded if I could find my way back."

"Not at all. I'm glad you got lost." She giggled, "I was getting bored. I was going to have some tea. Would you like some?"

"Yes, that would be great," David seemed more relaxed now. He needed a moment to digest all of this. He was not used to being astounded. In everyday life, he would rehearse every action down to the last mundane detail to avoid any surprises. But now, every second revealed a new, unexpected turn. Amanda was beautiful, dressed in a white overall that amplified her curves. And beyond that, she carried herself as if she was either oblivious to her beauty or comfortable with it.

She took his arm and guided him through one of the many passages that surrounded the entry to another room, where they sat next to a window with a view of the ocean. The fog cleared a few yards away from the house when seen from the top. This room was cozy and possessed a soothing blue hue.

Then, the same woman who had opened the door entered. She held a tray with a porcelain teapot and two cups and saucers.

Amanda poured some for both.

"Perhaps I should get back down on the trail."

"It will be dark soon. Would you like to stay for dinner? Would that be possible? I can arrange for you to return to your car after dinner," Amanda insisted.

David didn't know how to take this invitation. He didn't want to be surprised by her husband or boyfriend but didn't know how to express his concern. David asked, "Are you expecting somebody else?"

"No, I'm not," she answered with an expression of bewilderment. "I thought we could have wine, dinner, and a good conversation." She shook her head and shrugged.

"Sure, I just don't want your husband or significant other to be shocked by my presence. I know I wouldn't want to see a stranger in my house when I got home. Sorry if I'm being too explicit."

She laughed, "Oh, I get it. No, no, no, nothing like that." Now she was shaking her head vigorously from side to side, "I don't have a significant other. You don't need to worry about that." By now, she was laughing hard.

"Do you live here?" David asked and immediately thought it was a silly question. But on the other hand, this building did not feel like a house even though it looked like one.

"Sometimes—I travel a lot!"

He became preoccupied, thinking that maybe this was a sexual invitation. He was going to mention that he had a meeting at work but then decided to keep quiet. Nobody was waiting for him at home anyway. This situation was forcing him to be spontaneous. And he had a hard time doing that. But he decided not to reject her offer. "I don't want to impose," David said with a timid smile.

"Oh, don't be silly. You'll be doing me a favor. It would be boring if I had to have dinner all by myself. I'm glad you got lost today."

"What do you do up here? I mean, other than playing the organ?"

"I try to learn new things."

David asked curiously," What sort of things?"

"Things like music, food, sex."

"Oh, I see. Interesting you use the term *learn* for these," David said with amazement.

"They are experiences. But they have to be learned. At least, that is how it is for me."

"Is that all you do?" David asked.

"Oh, I also write about my experiences."

"Under what name do you publish? Perhaps I've heard of your work or even read one of your books."

Amanda replied, "I doubt that. I have just started writing."

"Are you planning to publish your work?"

"My first goal is to write. I can decide about publishing later. Does that interest you?" said Amanda.

"I write, too, primarily academic papers. I teach, and it looks good if I publish something once in a while."

"That is wonderful," she could hide her enthusiasm, "So, you are good at writing, then?"

"Well, there are different types of writing. I suppose I'm not too bad for what I do."

Amanda suggested, "Then I have a proposal for you. Would you be interested in participating in my research for my book?"

"What does the research involve?"

"I need to visit a few places, and I want to write about my experiences."

"How can I participate?"

"If you agree to accompany me, you will be well compensated, I assure you," Amanda said.

"That won't be necessary. But how do you know that you can trust me? I don't mean in terms of security but in opinion."

"I have a confession to make. We have this security system with built-in facial recognition, and when it warned me of your presence on the private road, it also gave me a synopsis of what you do and your writings. I'm sure you are a good fit to be my companion."

"Oh, that is a bit sudden! Maybe we can plan this for the next few weeks," said David.

"Can we talk about it after dinner? If you decide to stay, I can assure you that you will have an exceptional experience, and if you decide to leave, that is fine too. It would help if you simply accompanied me to a few events, and then we can discuss them later in casual conversations. That will complete my basic research. Ultimately, I will share a sample of my writing; you can critique it. And the pay is good, too."

Then, she completely changed the subject. "And for dinner, I have prepared something delicious I hoped to share with somebody. I want your opinion about it."

"But I'm not a food critic."

"You have had a lot of food before, I suppose, haven't you?"

"Oh yes, you bet." David could not hide a smile.

They walked to the dining room. Two maids, dressed in white overalls, similar to Amanda's, that now seemed like uniforms, smiled and ushered them to a beautifully decorated table with a bottle of uncorked red wine and two glasses. It was dark outside. Amanda asked, "What scenery would you like our table to be set in?" While she was pouring wine for both.

"You can do that?" asked David in amazement. "In that case, I leave it up to you."

"Oh yes, we have all kinds of things up here. I like the Sahara Desert scene for a change. I have seen enough of the ocean lately."

And immediately, their surroundings transformed into an oasis in a desert. Time was close to sunset on the screens, and when he paid close attention, he could see it was a live feed. He could feel the cool air of the desert at night. He could even smell the musky soil. David could not see any seams in the screens displaying the scene or any projectors. It was indeed an immersive experience. It was as if he was witnessing the view inside a VR headset, except there were no headsets. It seemed like the windows were made of a screen that could display any scenery at will or be transparent.

She then added, "It helps me get my experiences faster."

"This seems to be advanced technology you have here. I've never seen anything like it."

"I only use it as a tool. If it helps, it's good." She laughed.

"Is it made by the company you work for?"

"Company? What do you mean?" She seemed confused. "Companies are made to turn a profit. But that is not the purpose of the people I work with."

"I can't think of any other purpose for such advanced technology," said David.

Amanda smiled faintly, "How about those interested in acquiring knowledge?"

"You must mingle with people with much loftier goals than those I know who are trying to advance technology."

"I may tell you who my associates are at some point. But for now, let's just enjoy our dinner. Shall we? Can you tell me about yourself? You mentioned you write papers because you teach. Can you tell me more? What do you write about?"

"I teach engineering. It keeps me occupied," David responded. "I write about that stuff."

"Have you always been a teacher?"

"I used to work for a technology company, but I resigned. I needed more time to myself."

"Are you married?"

"I was… once," David sighed.

"Any kids?"

David responded briefly, "No," And shook his head.

"What happened to your marriage?"

David shrugged, "Same thing that happens to most marriages." Then he made a tight-lipped face, took a deep breath, and continued, "We got tired of each other. After that, I decided to do what I was passionate about." And drank some more wine.

There was silence for a while. Amanda then asked, "Do you have any questions for me?"

"I have many questions," David made a face as if he knew he would not get the answer, then poured some more wine for himself and offered some to Amanda.

Amanda shook her head, "I am good for the moment." Then she added calmly, "I would love to answer any questions you may have. But I just want to ask you to be patient. I don't want to be untruthful or deceptive. I can assure you that if you stay, your questions will be answered. But that is only if you stay. If you choose to leave, I am afraid I cannot answer many questions."

"And what if I decide to leave?..." asked David.

"Then you lose the chance to know. Based on what I have learned about you, you will be interested in my project. But it is really up to you." Amanda shrugged her shoulders and tilted her head.

"I'm fine with that. I haven't had a mystery in my life for a while. I'm beginning to think that maybe I should try this." David paused. He wanted to give the appearance that he respected Amanda's wish to learn more about her later. Still, David inadvertently asked questions that would complete Amanda's picture. "Let's talk about your fascination with music. Is that okay?"

"Oh, sure. I am fascinated by a lot of things, you will see. But you are right, music *is* fantastic. It is magical."

"You have the enthusiasm of somebody who is hearing music for the very first time," David noted.

"Music attracts me. Maybe because where I come from, music is not so central, let's say."

"Judging from your performance, it seems you have been familiar with music for a while," said David.

"Oh, I practice a lot. But it is always new to me." Amanda shook her head.

David felt that the more he asked, the more confused he became.

"Don't colleges in this area have a two-week recess? That gives you a good window to help me. *Please!*" Then she made an innocent face and closed her eyes, "*Please* be my assistant! It will only be for a few days." and took David's hands.

"You win. I will stay. It will be my pleasure."

Amanda's unbridled behavior broke all the rules. It forced David to act uncharacteristically spontaneously. Usually, he would consider the implications of staying at this house or whatever it was. *Nobody knows where I am,* he thought to himself. But what exactly could happen to him that would be unwanted? He wasn't a particularly wealthy individual. He had an apartment and worked at the local college. It would be hard to imagine a plot where somebody would ask for ransom for his release. Could the college be forced to negotiate a deal for his freedom if he was kidnapped? What could Amanda's motives be? "You leave me no choice," David smiled and shook his head. Amanda looked more beautiful and irresistible than before.

Amanda said, "I understand your hesitation. And believe me, if I was not sure of the opportunity this would bring you, I would not insist. You won't be disappointed; I can assure you."

But David was sensing an ulterior motive. "What is she after? Is this some sort of sexual alluring?" he asked himself. Despite his persistent reluctance, he couldn't detect whether she was happy that he was willing to take on an uncalculated risk and stay with her. However, what worked in Amanda's favor was that David's curiosity was piqued. He wanted to solve this puzzle. *Who was this woman, and what was this place?*

"You can stay the night in a bedroom alone or stay with me—your choice."

Again, this was unconventional, unbound, and, to the same degree, confusing to David. "Maybe tonight I will stay in a room alone," David answered with hesitation and a hint of disbelief. Was he reading too much into this?

"It wasn't a sexual suggestion. You don't need to worry about that. I only want us to share bedtime. I know that is a special time for most people."

David replied quickly, "And some people enjoy that time alone. I hope I have not offended you."

"No offense taken. But out of curiosity, what is the requirement for sleeping together in one bed?"

"Well, we just met. You don't even know if I have a companion. Sleeping together is an intimate thing, at least for me." Said David.

"Are you implying that staying together needs to be sexual?"

David mumbled, "It increases the possibility!"

"Only if you want it to—in any case, that was just a suggestion. I can assure you the experience of staying here and spending time with me will be worth the trouble." She immediately said, "How about a walk in the garden," as if to change the subject altogether.

"I'd love it."

She guided him through a door to a Japanese-style garden. They walked on a bridge over a pond where he could hear the koi splash. There was a temple on the right side of the gravel-laid road that led to the bridge. Amanda stepped inside, sounded the bell, closed her eyes, and stood silently, arms crossed over her chest. David felt a burning desire to hold and kiss her but restrained himself.

His attention was drawn to the sky, which seemed to have more stars than he was used to.

He felt that was strange, but by this time, he was mired in this adventure with many little snippets that felt odd and misplaced. Were these intentional clues, and if so, to what?

"Are you a religious person?" he asked.

"What makes you say that?"

"I saw your eyes were closed, and it seemed like you were praying or meditating."

"Well, that is part of the experience, too. I want to see what it is like to be a person of faith," Amanda replied.

"So, you have no beliefs of your own?"

"Nothing supernatural. I can't say that I *believe* in anything. To me, belief implies adherence to an idea despite evidence to the contrary. And in that sense, I am a non-believer." And she smiled.

"You talk like a philosopher."

Amanda replied, "More like a realist, I would say."

"Can I ask you something?"

"Yes, please," Amanda said.

"What if somebody else had walked through that door today? Would you have shown the same interest?"

Amanda answered calmly, "That would depend on the person. Maybe. If I felt they could be a good assistant for my research, why not."

"So, you think I should believe that it was just the luck of the draw that you were looking for an assistant, and I showed up, and you felt that could be me?"

Amanda said, "I think there is always a chance of something serendipitous happening any day, don't you? Also, when I asked you, it wasn't simply based on a gut feeling."

"So, you have investigated me?" David asked abruptly.

"I already told you about the facial recognition system and the information it provided. Once I realized you were published, I decided to circumvent my search and try you for this position. Otherwise, I would need to go through an arduous selection process, arrange for interviews, and bring people in for final selection, and in the end, the result would not have been any better. So, it was simply a lucky coincidence that I could offer you the spot. You can still refuse. It would make me sad, but you can," Amanda said with such a deep gaze into David's eyes that he had no choice but to accept the explanation.

"Don't you feel that is a bit intrusive?"

Amanda answered, "We all better get used to that! Whether we like it or not, we are recognized and analyzed all the time. You could say we are all celebrities now. We all now live in the public eye."

How could David believe that this was all just a chance encounter? On the other hand, what else could it be? He hadn't felt any coaxing to decide to go for a hike today. He'd only diverted from his usual path a little. Otherwise, this was his regular route. He'd always wanted to go up a little farther on that trail, but he'd always postponed it, and today, he felt, was the right time. He had even argued that it was a good day to try it because he would be tired after the hike but could recuperate the following days since college would be in recess. And even when the fog settled in, it wasn't enough to dissuade him. What was the nature of this adventure? How was it that his uneventful life suddenly held the prospect of all this excitement? Beyond the possibility of these events being part of a plot, there was also the question of motivation. *Why* would anybody *want* to deceive him? Or could he just accept it as a coincidence? He knew about other instances where a chance event had led someone to invent something, join a venture, or even fall in love with someone. Maybe this was one of those situations.

***

That night, when David arrived at his room, a vast space with a balcony overhanging from the edge of the cliff, and prepared for bed, a voice asked if he wanted to experience any specific effects in his sleeping quarters. He requested that his bed be placed on a rooftop in Tehran to recreate the summer nights his father had told him about in many bedtime stories. The experience was more natural and nuanced than he expected. The cool breeze would stop from time to time to reveal the dry heat of the night. He could hear the neighborhood cats running along the ledges. He could also hear the occasional car cruising down the street. The night had a serenity he had not felt in a long time. Everything could be experienced rather than told. This was the ultimate display of concepts, which gave him a window into precisely who Amanda was—the *ultimate observer*. And now he, David, was becoming an observer too. He understood this to be the main takeaway from this *chance* encounter. And now he was truly intrigued to follow this maze to the end.

The Morning Run

Early the following day, the whole room was lit with sunshine. David could not see the sun or what was causing this effect, but it appeared that some sort of active simulation was still depicting the city in the morning—more car noises and the hum of the town with faint voices of the passers-by. He sat in bed and immersed himself in the moment, feeling the uncomfortable warmth of the sun. Sparrows were flying overhead so close that one would be tempted to extend their arm and catch them. This was not any kind of technology David was familiar with. Although all indications were that the reality was interactive, what he did was ask it to end, "End simulation." That was enough to return the room to the state before the simulation started.

Now David could see the stairs at the end of the balcony through the bedroom glass doors. He assumed they led to the beach. David went inside the room to put on his hiking boots, only to notice a pair of running shoes beside them. He put them on instead. They were a perfect fit.

He went to the balcony, followed it to the end, and onto the stairs heading down. After a few steps, the staircase entered a vertical tunnel with a small opening in the middle and the stairs spiraling around the perimeter of it, like an enclosed inverted tower. It was as if they had bored a hole into the bedrock and mounted the staircase around the center of it. There were no railings. Doubt set in for a second, but David continued descending the stairs for a period that felt like many hours. He went toward the edge and looked up cautiously to see the opening to the balcony to gauge the distance he had traveled, and it did seem far away. Somehow, he knew he should continue. The staircase was poorly lit. To avoid the sense of vertigo, he leaned on the right side of the shaft and continued the descent. Eventually, a patch of light appeared, and David emerged and found himself on the beach. He looked up and saw the house, close to the clouds, it seemed. Maybe it was enough of an adventure for one day, but he was intrigued to see if he could find anybody else on the beach.

He started his run. It felt like one of those days when he could run for miles. He removed his shoes and left them on one of the big rocks. He wanted to feel the wet sand on his feet. He noticed that the beach seemed different than the one he was on before starting his hike up the trail the day before.

After running for about an hour, he had still not encountered a single person. He became alarmed and turned back. He ran as fast as he could and began to worry that he might be lost. He had no idea what to expect if that happened. He was relieved when he found the rock where he'd left his shoes. Then he looked for the staircase. Luckily, he found it with no problem and started climbing. A few minutes later, he saw an exit from the tunnel, and in his anxiety, he immediately took it. But this was a different access than the one he had entered on the way down. A few seconds later, he saw Amanda standing on the balcony, naked. It was too late for him to turn around. He felt embarrassed, but it didn't seem like she did. She started talking, which forced him to look at her.

Amanda asked, "How was the run?"

"I'm so sorry; I didn't know the stairs would lead to your room," David was trying to avoid eye contact with Amanda and pretended that everything was normal.

Amanda answered, "That's fine. Don't you like my body? I love it! I can feel the breeze on my whole body. That is an interesting experience. Don't you think?"

"I guess I've always taken it for granted. But come to think of it, it is pretty cool to feel the breeze."

"Would you like to feel it?" Amanda offered.

David answered, astonished, "You mean your body? Oh no, I'd prefer to take a shower now. I've been running for quite a while."

Amanda asked, "Do you feel embarrassed?"

"That too. But right now, I just want to shower."

"Aren't you aroused to see my body?" she asked with an innate innocence.

David wasn't sure how to answer.

She then said, "Suit yourself…! You can go to your room from here." She pointed to the hallway. "Or you can take a shower in my room."

"Thank you. I guess I'll go to my room and shower there," David uttered.

"We have a full schedule today. I have asked my people to put out proper attire for you. Just look in the closet."

***

After showering, David got dressed and opened the bedroom door. The suit, shirt, and shoes were again a perfect fit. One of Amanda's coworkers was waiting outside his bedroom door and guided him to the living room, where David found Amanda dressed in black.

Amanda asked, "How do you like my dress?"

"It is very nice," said David. But he couldn't erase Amanda's naked figure from his head. The perfect breasts and the shape of her waistline were ingrained in his mind.

"Oh, I know what you are thinking. But be careful. We are invited to a funeral today. You have to behave," Amanda giggled.

Then, one of the workers brought a silver box. Amanda opened it and said, "You have to try this. It is great." In the box was a skin-colored round coin the size of a penny. "Put it on anywhere behind your ear, and we will be able to share our experiences."

He did.

"Now we can share thoughts and visions…"

David turned around in mid-sentence and stared at Amanda. Her lips were not moving, but the voice was indistinguishable. This was the first test of the device.

"All you need to do is to decide to share, and the device will do it automatically. And if you want absolute privacy, simply remove the device and put it back in the silver box." Amanda's thoughts were streaming into his mind effortlessly.

Realities

The entry of the house led to many hallways. Each hallway was lined up with many doors that looked alike. David wanted but did not ask `about the purpose of so many hallways and doors. Instead, he decided to let time explain all of that.

Amanda held David's arm, guided him to one of the many doors, and opened it. They entered a busy street. Amanda said, "I will try to use the MAC device only as needed. Soon, you will become used to the difference between when my thoughts are transmitted and when I talk. Oh, MAC stands for multi-access communication. It helps the user experience a full immersion into a certain reality."

"I always thought there was only one reality," David's expression changed to incredulity.

Amanda responded, "You have a lot to learn, David. Reality is in the eye of the beholder!" She said this with utter indifference and immediately continued, "Let's have some croissants and coffee. I know this little shop." She pulled his hand and led him to a storefront where the smell of freshly baked bread and coffee was overwhelming. They sat at a table.

Amanda asked, "Are you having a good time so far?"

"Yes, I think I'm getting used to this reality," David said with a grin.

"How serious are you about running?" asked Amanda.

"I started running in my early teens. It turned into a habit, and now I am addicted to it, you can say. Maybe I should slow down a bit. I'm not as young anymore."

Amanda changed the subject abruptly again, "Remind me to take you to this local music café later. I can't wait for us to go there. They have some very talented players—but later. Not today. Today, we will be busy."

A Funeral

They went through a glass door and a bright passage and then took an elevator to the roof of the building.

Within a few seconds, a large drone appeared and landed. The doors opened automatically to reveal a very comfortable interior and no pilot. David could not see the standard controls and gauges he expected to see in a plane.

Once they settled, Amanda told David, "It knows where we are going."

As far as David could tell, it was some sort of a quiet jet. The closest thing he had seen before was a quadcopter, except this one had no visible propellers. The drone soared. From there, David could see that they were flying over an island and thought he was entirely lost because that contradicted his memory of where he expected the house to be. The experience of being in the drone was like being in an elevator. He hadn't been exposed to any details that revealed how it flew. Amanda asked David to relax and assured him the craft would take them where they were supposed to go.

The drone approached a tall building and landed precisely within a demarcated area. David and Amanda got off. The doors automatically closed behind them like a clamshell, and the drone flew away.

They entered an elevator directly into a vast auditorium a few floors below. This was where the events for Patrick's company, Star Commercial Realty, or SCR for short, took place. And today, Patrick's body was laid to rest in a massive open casket at the top of the room. It looked like a capsule meant to be sent into space rather than one that was supposed to be buried.

This did not exactly seem like a religious gathering. Champagne, pastries, and various hors d'oeuvres were being served. Amanda introduced David to a few people who surrounded her when they arrived.

Frederick was SCR's VP of Operations. He also played the role of a close friend. This combination put him at the center of the details of the ceremony. Since Patrick had no family, at least as far as the company knew, the whole business of the memorial service and funeral, usually handled by the family, had become a company affair. When he saw Amanda, he pulled her to a corner. It was as if he had seen his therapist or his best friend. Finally, there was somebody to confide in. After all, it would have been odd for him to complain to anybody else.

He started anxiously, visibly annoyed, "I don't know where to begin. Patrick had a special way of running this business, leaving many things in limbo with little hierarchy. Information was only provided as needed, as if he was running some secret agency."

The company had no effective board of directors, and none of the managers knew anything about the operations besides what they oversaw directly. And now they had no playbook to follow. It was as if Patrick had never existed.

Frederick continued, "We have been unable to get into Patrick's computer since it is password protected. Also, we discovered that many critical files on servers were encrypted, and we don't have the decryption keys. I knew I should have asked, but I was not resolute enough, and he resisted documenting all critical passwords and encryption keys. Of course, this did not cause any issues while he was around. He showed up at 5:30 every morning and prepared a list of instructions for the managers. Even when he was on various trips, he was accessible electronically. Hence, we never encountered any problems that would reveal how critical the information only he had access to was. He was not married, nor did he have any kids. He talked about a brother sometimes, but no one had ever seen him or had any contact with him. I wish there was somebody who could take over. We can run the company. No problem there. I just don't know where things stand legally. And how to deal with taxes and so on. I'm hiring a computer security firm to investigate the situation of the encrypted files. We may have to go to court to figure out all this."

A lack of family and close friends had not prevented Patrick from amassing a vast fortune. He owned many properties and many businesses associated with those properties. He had built his empire piece by piece through acquisitions facilitated by relationships he had developed with council members in various towns and municipalities.

When a company went bankrupt, and a building was abandoned, municipalities had a problem. Patrick went to the rescue. There was an intricate balance between what banks allowed, and city governments wanted. For Patrick, the cost of entry was meager, and the only risk was if his refurbishments did not find a suitable buyer. Patrick became involved with many small businesses as the sole owner or partner. His empire was diversified. He hired a team of people to help him manage his vast holdings. This building, where they were gathered today, was where it all happened. His leaders acted like copies of Patrick but reported only to him. He was indeed a ventriloquist with global tentacles, and he kept it all straight in a brain that was used to complexity.

But beyond the money he generated, he did not seem to have done much else. No wife, no kids, no family, and no charity work. The only thing he was famous for was going to

Vegas once a month and playing high-stakes blackjack. Some said he had won a lot, and some claimed he broke even. Whatever the case, it was clear that casinos were pleased to see him.

Some believed he must have secretly helped many families, but nobody knew for sure. They did not know about his religious views or his political affiliation. None of them were even sure about his level of education; he had never mentioned any alma maters. For all they knew, he might have been a high school dropout. But even that was not clear. He spread the details of his life like grains of sand among them. As a result, many people knew a lot of information but not in a cohesive manner. They knew he was born in the Midwest and had moved to Boston when he was young. He had multiple houses in Manhattan, Miami, Los Angeles, and Seattle and divided his free time equally between those cities—and Las Vegas.

This was information that Patrick had mentioned in passing. He did not like to be questioned about details. As soon as someone asked questions beyond what he'd volunteered, he would go silent, sometimes hours before he started talking again.

In reality, it turned out that the person his friends considered close to them was a total stranger. Everyone knew bits and pieces, but nobody seemed to know the whole story.

Patrick was not fond of big crowds and was accompanied by a small entourage to all events he attended, rotating the people in that group. They felt obliged to say goodbye and pay their respects when they heard about his passing. Frederick, who had organized the event, could not give it a unifying theme because he was torn between what he thought was appropriate and what Patrick would have wanted since nobody had a firm grasp of Patrick's life story.

Even the circumstances surrounding his death seemed tenuous, although it had occurred in broad daylight and public view when he was playing golf with a few friends. They saw him going into a sand trap to hit the ball. They saw the ball fly away, but David never emerged. When they went to check on him, they found him facedown with a mouthful of sand, eyes still open, and the club clutched in both hands. He was not breathing. A few people tried to resuscitate him to no avail, and when paramedics arrived, they pronounced him dead on the scene.

Some speculated that he might have arranged his death. He certainly seemed like a man with such desires. It felt as if he was still alive somewhere, just in an altered state. Was the dead body an actor? Was Patrick trying to divert attention and escape his increasingly complex obligations and relationships?

Nevertheless, Frederick had decided they needed to arrange a final farewell gathering. Frederick struggled with whether the service required to follow the beliefs of the person for whom it was being held. And precisely who determined what those beliefs were? Since Patrick did not seem to have any family, Frederick had become the deciding party, but he felt he didn't know Patrick well after all. And even though there was no indication that Patrick was religious, Frederick had felt that there should be at least some aspects of a religious ceremony, "just in case." And that was why Father Francis was there. Francis claimed he'd had long conversations with Patrick and warned him about going through life without direction and just accumulating wealth.

Father Francis's eulogy was a mix of his usual sermon and reminiscing conversations he'd had with Patrick over the years. "We all need to go someday. That we know. The only question is how we get from birth to death, from point A to point B. Today is inevitable; death is inevitable. But it is not the end; life is not a straight line. That is why we need the Lord's authority to navigate our path. And that is why we need the laws of morality. The afterlife is eternal, while life is limited and mired in agony, disease, and disaster. We are tested and prepared here for eternal life after death; we will continue in the afterlife; we need to. Otherwise, life would be meaningless. What we do here defines how we will continue there."

"I know that Patrick was not particularly religious," Francis sighed. "But I am confident of one thing: that he was saved and that he was a moral man. The fact that we are all here is indicative of that. We were his family. He was good to all of us. I am sure that he also helped the needy as he saw fit. As far as I know, he only had one request: to be buried under this building. One of his first improvements in this building was constructing a vault. And I must say that I had completely forgotten about it until I learned of his passing, which jogged my memory. I mentioned the vault in my conversation with Frederick and Patrick's specific request he'd made almost two years ago. He used to ask me many questions about death and the purpose of life. And I answered them to the best of my ability."

"I was hoping he would one day attend a Sunday service, but that never happened. Instead, he would invite me to his house for dinner, and our conversations were held during friendly games of cards and drinking wine. I often hoped he would confide in me about any issues, but that did not happen either. Until one day, he told me about the vault and his desire to be buried there. And I sensed that he was telling me this as an executor of his wish. I naturally thought it was not a good idea for him to tell me this since I was his senior by a couple of decades. He never told me about his family, where he went to school, or what he did before moving here. But I felt obligated to make sure his wish came true, and indeed, when Frederick and I went to the vault, we found detailed instructions about his wishes for the burial."

About one hundred friends had gathered. Other than Father Francis, two other guests got up to talk. One of them was Steven, a portly man, about fifty. Not a comfortable public speaker, it was evident that he felt a debt of gratitude that he needed to express. "I ran into Patrick accidentally, but it changed my life forever. I own a small parking operation in Vegas. One night, he was quite drunk, and I gave him a ride to his hotel. He made it a point to find me the next day and gave me a generous tip. He then asked if I wanted to be his valet. He told me that he knew he could trust me. I was to be available when he arrived in Vegas and would take him anywhere, and everywhere he wanted to go. He hired a manager to run my business so I could spend more time finding him unique places to go. He gave me a salary twice as much as my profit from the business. In addition, every time he came to Vegas and gambled, I got a tip equal to 15% of all he spent. I didn't keep track, but I trusted him. He wanted to have a good time without being concerned about his safety. That was valuable to him. For me, it meant an extra 200K a year. And that was valuable to me. So, a good deal overall. As far as I was concerned, he was doing me a favor. He could have done it by spending much less, but I think he valued loyalty."

Attendees were visibly surprised and in awe of Patrick's generosity, which seemed excessive given his attention to saving in all aspects of business operations.

The other one to speak was George, a fit man with a shaved head and pronounced facial features. He looked like a person with a military background: confident and authoritative. It was unclear whether he shaved his head to "hide" a bald spot or to go with his physique and demeanor. However, he was much more soft-spoken and articulate than his appearance revealed.

***

As Amanda was talking to Frederick, George interjected to ask Frederick about some details of the ceremony. Frederick introduced George, and it was revealed that George also helped set up the gathering and encouraged Frederick to follow a few religious rituals.

"With all due respect, how did you conclude that Patrick would want a religious service like this?" Amanda asked George.

"I was not sure about it, but I felt some rituals had to be followed. I think Religion is a go-to place for fast and quick advice, especially when it comes to rituals. You see, my take on religion is different from most people's. I don't consider it true whether God truly said such or whether following a religion brings us eternal happiness. I think religion is a collection of beliefs humans have made up over thousands of years to help us cope with things bigger than us: death, birth, and marriage—believe me, I know—I've done it three times already. We all know religion is nonsense, but we still need it. Relatives and close friends are so distraught when someone close passes away that nobody has time to think, let alone come up with a format for a ceremony. That's why it is simply easier to follow the religious ones, especially in this case because it turned out that he wished to be buried in the basement of this building in a vault, which would have been weird to do without some type of ceremony. That was the only thing that anybody knew of his wishes. Patrick was a very private person. Don't get me wrong, he was outgoing and talkative but did not let anyone in. We each thought that surely there must be someone who knew him well, but when we all gathered under one roof, it became clear that none of us was that person," George responded.

***

After the speakers, all guests gathered in the open space of the auditorium—wine, champagne, beer, and for those who needed something more potent, whiskey or other heavy alcoholic drinks were served.

Amanda, George, Frederick, Francis, and Steven were engaged in a lively discussion about Patrick. George said, "I have never met anybody who lived so much for the moment. He never talked about his past or why he was adamant about enjoying the moment. I accompanied him on many trips and did a few thrilling things with him, including extreme skiing, where a helicopter drops you off onto a slope, or base jumping, sky diving, you name it. He even tried climbing Mt. Everest, but the expedition ended with four deaths. He could not wait to try it again; it was on his agenda. Thrill-seeking was what he lived for."

Francis interjected, "I believe he must have been concerned about life after death. Otherwise, why would he have arranged for his body to be kept frozen underneath this building?"

Frederick added, "To him, life was not simply for enjoyment but for experiencing. He wanted to know what it meant to climb Mt. Everest, jump from a building, or be able to literally fly with artificial wings. I don't think Patrick simply did it for the thrill. He might have even feared death, but he didn't let his fear be an obstacle. At least, that is my take. He downplayed the danger of many extreme activities when I raised concerns. I was too timid to ask for complete access to all information, fearing he might take it the wrong way and think I was planning a takeover of the operation. Once, I asked him to leave instructions to help us operate in his absence. Do you know his answer? 'That would jinx my trip.' He was a little superstitious that way. And, of course, none of those dangerous activities brought him any harm. Who would have thought? A healthy man, a very healthy man, would die while playing golf, the most docile of activities. And he only played to mingle with business owners to increase sales, you know. He didn't really like golf. What a waste. I'm afraid he left this empire for the government to take over. If we can't make heads or tails of this operation, we have no choice but to shut it down. All the bank accounts are in his name. I have access to some funds but not nearly enough to run this behemoth for long."

Amanda said, "Let's say he married or had kids. Would that have changed any of his experiences? He realized life was limited, and the most you could hope for was to experience what was available to you, which he did."

George chuckled, "He could have experienced divorce! That would have changed his perspective. Maybe he tried sharing his life and was unsuccessful. Maybe somebody betrayed him at some point, so he decided to go through life solo."

Francis looked thoughtful, "You don't just do everything in life for the sake of experience. Lord has made marrying and having children enjoyable because they are meant to replenish the earth. That's God's glory. If we don't marry, it should be for a higher cause, such as dedicating your life to spreading the word of the Lord."

George challenged, "I doubt Patrick was motivated by the word of God. He might have believed something, but it wasn't in any organized religion. I remember he used a lot of analogies to express his outlook on life. The one that sticks in my mind the most is: "You are born with a set of chips in hand. You can play any game you want. But remember, eventually, you will lose all your chips because the house always wins. Some people lose their chips sooner than the rest, but we all lose them, no doubt. In the end, we take the memory of the games we played—the moments, nothing more. You can spend your day any way you want, but remember you have paid some chips to spend your days a certain way. Just make sure what you take away is worth the chips you spent."

Eventually, it was time for the main event. George selected six men from the audience to be the pallbearers. The casket looked heavy and well-built to protect its contents. They carried it to the service elevator, holding it and not setting it down. The rest of the attendees lined up to take the main elevators to the basement. The basement was a long corridor with three doors and five elevator entrances. A double door that had remained closed until today was now open. The vault was inside this room. The vault that would hold Patrick's coffin looked like those generally seen at banks, with heavy bars and a big wheel used to close it tightly. George was already facing the vault. He entered a code on a keypad to open it.

At the crescent-shaped room entrance that housed hundreds of computer servers, a music ensemble had gathered and was playing Bach's Agnus Dei from the Mass in B Minor.

Thousands of files on the servers that defined Patrick's business had probably been rendered useless with his death. A person who had left many unanswered questions had carefully choreographed his burial with as much detail as possible.

Once the door opened, the six men entered and placed the casket on a pedestal. Then, one of the men opened the coffin's viewing port as if to assure everyone that he was indeed there. The audience lined up as each person entered the vault, bowed, turned around, and came out. Patrick's face was calm, and it looked like he would wake up anytime.

When everybody had paid their respects, George closed the viewing port and the vault door and pressed a button. He murmured, "Goodbye, my friend." Then he turned and announced, "The vault will now be vacuumed and air sealed.

Its temperature will be controlled to a constant −40°C. The building has self-sustaining power to provide the energy needed to preserve Patrick for eternity!"

It was getting late, and it was time to leave. Moments later, Amanda and David found the drone waiting for them where it had dropped them off. The drone soared as soon as they entered it. The building was now desolate. Only Patrick stayed. Safe and frozen.

David could not wait to ask Amanda, "How did you know Patrick?"

"He was a recent acquaintance. Let's say we ran into each other. We had some interesting conversations," Amanda almost whispered.

"About what?" asked David.

"About everything—music, philosophy, literature. Patrick was a well-rounded man and, as far as I know, self-taught. He didn't take anything lightly. Patrick was intense. He was passionate about everything he pursued," Amanda maintained a somber mood.

David could not hide the humorous tone and said, "How did you exactly run into him? Was he hiking on the trail at some point?"

Amanda looked at David with a vague smile or maybe a smirk; he couldn't tell which. She then took his hands. "You know, I'm beginning to like you."

When they returned to the house, Amanda invited David to dinner at a local restaurant. They stepped out of one of the numerous doors, which David was beginning to believe were gateways or portals of some sort. They found themselves on a street that looked like it was located in a small Italian town.

Once they settled at the sidewalk table, Amanda asked, "What do you think was the oddest thing about today's ceremony?"

David responded, "Maybe Patrick himself. I've heard of people who want to experience the moment, but at least in the case of Patrick, it had some heavy consequences. The fact that he would allow what he built to face the risk of being dismantled so easily was striking. I think maybe he knew what he was doing."

"You mean he did it intentionally, or was he just careless?" Amanda asked.

"He couldn't have been careless. I am unsure if he meant to leave no legacy. Maybe he underestimated the value of what he left behind and how it affected other people's lives. At some point, it is not your legacy anymore," David said deliberately.

Amanda asked, "Why do you think a person's legacy is important?"

"Maybe because that is what makes our short lives matter. People still talk about Alexander the Great, Genghis Khan, Newton, and Einstein. It's all about legacy, isn't it?".

"Do you think Genghis Khan was concerned about his legacy or simply cared about his immediate family or maybe his tribe?"

"No religion or nationality lives in a vacuum—these entities are expressed through individuals who hope to be recognized. They want to matter and be remembered as having mattered. That is where legacy comes into play: to transcend time and mortality. When we see someone who deviates from this path, it surprises us. And I think Patrick was just such a person and interesting because of it," David concluded.

A Birthday Party

Amanda asked, "Do you like birthday parties?"

"Not particularly."

"But this one is interesting. I think you are going to like it. I want you to come with me," Amanda insisted.

"Do I have a choice?" asked David.

"It would defeat the purpose of the experience if you didn't attend. If you're not going, I won't go either—but it should be interesting,"

She opened the main entrance, and they walked outside. It was sunny and mildly warm. They waited near the fountain. A car appeared with no driver. David did not recognize the brand even though he considered himself a car enthusiast. He did not comment on the vehicle. He got in, and Amanda sat next to him. Inside, it looked like a luxurious train cabin. There were no obvious control mechanisms, no pedals or steering wheel. She held his hand and told him she was delighted he accompanied her to the birthday party. David asked how Amanda knew the hosts, to which she replied, "I know a lot of people."

They were driven for about 15 minutes. The car cruised down a narrow, winding road, skillfully handling the sharp turns. David asked Amanda if these cars were available on the market, and she told him that not all he saw was in the market. The vehicle went through a gate, entered a long driveway, and stopped at a compound of multiple villa-style buildings, complete with a multilevel fountain.

It appeared to be a red-carpet reception. Amanda got out of the car first, and David followed. They entered the main house. Everybody knew Amanda. David felt out of place and was unsure how to conduct himself even though the other guests were warm to him.

Clark was the host, tall and very fit and confident. Next to him was Alison, his wife, beautiful and slim and appeared to be in her thirties. They approached Amanda, and each hugged and kissed her. Amanda introduced David as her friend and assistant.

Amanda asked Clark, "I hear you were in a triathlon last week. Is that right?"

"You know me. I die for these things even though they border on torture. But I like the concept. You have to overcome a lot, and I like a challenge. It helps me with what I have to face in business," Clark responded.

Then Alison set the tone for the evening, "I'm glad I didn't have to give birth. It ruins your figure. I cannot imagine how some women do it only because they want children."

Amanda sensed David's curiosity and confusion and pointed out, "Clark is the founder of BioTechnitos, the company that plans to revolutionize the whole birth process and maybe even parenting. It will disrupt the norms and the way we look at things. Women will be able to have children without any of the normal difficulties: pregnancy and giving birth, birth defects, and inherited diseases. And there is a bonus: parents can choose what features their kids will have—from the color of their skin to how tall they are—perfect vision and heart and all of that. And you know, Clark is not just the CEO; he is a client, too."

Clark smiled, "We had to set an example. People need to see that we don't just preach it. We wanted kids, and we thought this was the best way. We wanted two girls and one boy, which is exactly what we have."

Alison added, "I was not too fond of the idea of having kids at first. But it was mostly because of my unease with the childbirth process. There is nothing wrong with having kids once giving birth is eliminated."

David was astonished, "Wow, that seems radical. Then who carries the fetus?"

"Nobody—it is implanted in an artificial womb!" Alison said triumphantly.

"God knows how much productivity is lost due to the childbearing process," Clark quickly added.

"How about the bond that they say exists between mother and child, which is supposedly because of the birthing process and the length of time that the baby feels her mother's heartbeat and so forth?" David, who was now glad to have accepted this visit, uttered enthusiastically.

Clark responded, "All our animal tests have shown no difference between how a mother treats her kids when they are born naturally versus through the AW-that is the acronym for artificial womb. It also did not cause any behavioral differences in children. I might add that we see this through first-hand experience in our kids. They bond with their mom just fine and don't act weird."

Alison asked, "Have you seen an artificial womb?". Then she continued, "They are very much biological and are created through DNA extraction. They are like the natural womb, except that they lack all imperfections. The AW is what a perfect womb should be. It is perfect. They even add natural sounds and external stimuli during incubation. The AW is a whole system. It is not just one thing."

"And they make perfect kids!" Amanda muttered.

Alison and Clark announced they would check on the kids and headed to the "children's" side of the house.

A man approached Amanda with a big smile. Amanda hugged him, turned to David, and introduced him, "This is Dr. Rosenstein; we call him the Father of the Designer Kids."

Dr. Rosenstein, a short and slightly overweight man with balding hair, was probably not a designer kid himself. He was accompanied by a slender woman with short, blond hair and round glasses who was introduced as Alexandria Petrovsky, the mother of the artificial womb. They were in the heat of an argument just before they saw Amanda and decided to say hi.

Then Rosenstein decided to continue the discussion, now in the presence of Amanda and David, "Ultimately, I think, if an invention makes life easier, people tend to use it and wonder about the social ramifications of it only after they have used it. I don't see why we shouldn't use this technology."

"Maybe because the implications are grave. Maybe because many ethical and moral issues need to be addressed, and maybe because humans are not yet equipped to answer them," responded Petrovsky.

Rosenstein was now visibly excited and was using his hands to prove a point, "That could be said about all human inventions. It is well-known that the Greeks were concerned about losing their memory skills when writing was invented."

"But you know this issue goes to the heart of equality in a society and the creation of a superhuman race," Petrovsky replied immediately.

Rosenstein argued, "We can't fix everything. We are a technology company."

Petrovsky replied, "And that is precisely why regulations are needed to limit its use. An artificial womb is one thing, but modifying human DNA is another level of intervention."

Rosenstein seemed frustrated and excited at the same time, "Where do you draw the line? The use of an AW is as unnatural as modifying human DNA. And historically, if we can do something, regulations will follow. Human history is all about intervention in nature. Everything around us is artificial: agriculture, construction, medicine, language."

"The only thing comparable is the use of nuclear power. Do you think it could have been used without heavy regulations? Listen, humans are becoming more and more powerful, and their decisions will increasingly have serious consequences. This is about a fundamental change in the structure of society. It should not be reduced to a business and profiteering decision," Petrovsky declared with a deliberately slow pace.

David entered the discussion, "The more interesting question is why people who profit from a practice also tend to believe it is ethical. Do they pretend, or does their judgment get affected by their interests? Why do we feel the need to follow moral values or ethical norms at all? Could we be just trying to convince others that we are ethical because we need their approval? With all due respect, Dr. Rosenstein, it appears that you are biased towards using this technology and willing to overlook many issues that could be raised."

Rosenstein was surprised but tried to keep his cool. "The only ethical question is whether everyone has access to it. I don't think we have an obligation or a pact with nature. We don't even know how to approach that question."

"But maybe we should. This is just the beginning of the road. If humans can alter nature this deeply, maybe they should also have a pact with nature," Amanda said.

Petrovsky acted like a scientist who had contributed to creating the atomic bomb but was now unhappy with the unintended consequences of what she had done. In her mind, AW had medical benefits, but she could see its drawbacks.

A tall man with nicely combed silver hair in a dark blue suit, right out of the GQ Magazine, approached. Next to him was a familiar face—Father Francis. "My name is Robert Olen. I overheard your conversation. May I say a few words?"

Father Francis said, "Amanda, it is good to see you again. It seems like our paths are crossing a lot these days."

Rosenstein acknowledged Olen, "By all means. This is a new field; the more we hear, the better. By the way, I'm familiar with your work, Dr. Olen."

Olen started, "There are several problems with how things are concerning childbirth: first, there is the downtime for parents. Then there is the issue of uncertainty about the health of the newborn, and finally, there is the issue of raising the child, which right now is a private matter. And more importantly, there are no laws governing the levels of population. Besides the danger of overpopulation and scarcity of resources, we are increasingly faced with irrelevant people who can't make meaningful contributions to society. We have brushed these issues under the rug for a long time, but they will come back to haunt us eventually. Advances in technology are making the need for high levels of population unnecessary. Let's remember how we got here. In agrarian societies, people had children because they believed their livelihood depended on it. They made many babies, anticipating they would lose a few before they came of age. Then, in the industrial society, populations were needed to man the factories. If you look at the population levels, you will notice that we have inadvertently been replenishing the human infrastructure of society. The history of the human race is the history of the self-domestication of humans. We may have thought we were making babies in pursuit of happiness, but we have just been contributing to preserving the human resources needed to move society forward. However, here comes something out of the left field: Throughout history, if you were able-bodied and willing, you could find work. We are increasingly moving toward an era where swaths of people are being rendered superfluous, pure and simple. Some jobs have already vanished. As for the remaining, we can imagine that some sort of machine could soon perform them. Some people can be retrained, but most will become irrelevant—forever. The question then becomes, what are we going to do with the existing populaces, and what will we do with the population levels moving forward? Our best hope is that people automatically act as if they are applying market notions to reproduction. Reproduce less now because less is needed. Of course, it is better if reproduction is handled by other means, something different than the nuclear family model, pregnancy, childbirth, etc. But I'm also very wary of large-scale social engineering. Whatever it is, we need to lure people into controlling population growth voluntarily."

Petrovsky was now visibly alarmed, "Are you suggesting that having children artificially should replace the natural way and that governments should decide population levels?!"

Olen replied calmly, "I am not suggesting that they should. I'm simply saying that they will, inevitably. At some point, we must determine what defines us as humans. Are we humans because we procreate? And what is the function of each individual? Being human increasingly means being able to define how we live and the quality of life we establish for ourselves. The more we leave these issues to chance, the farther away we get from being human."

"I think what Mr. Olen brought up is important and another aspect of why regulating matters affecting the lives of large population segments is necessary. I don't favor regulation from a bureaucratic point of view, but we need social supervision and contemplation before we commit to a method that could affect our lives so deeply. Even then, we cannot guarantee that there will not be any problems," Amanda exclaimed.

"Another aspect is whether we are dealing with corporate greed or real improvement in people's lives. Shouldn't that be our guide?" David asked.

"It's not just that; we need to prepare for the future. At some point, we have to decide how and when to add members to society. This should not be left to chance. The AW is a move in the right direction to address this. This cannot be left to a social structure, like marriage, that is crumbling," Said Olen.

"May I remind you that no past social experimentation has had good results! New methods should not be forced. They should be embraced instead. What you are suggesting is profound and will change the face of humanity forever," David said softly, trying to be polite.

Rosenstein didn't wait, "But if we don't try, we will never know. Change is inevitable, and this is the path placed before us. We have violated nature in the past from the dawn of time. From makeup and dying of hair and false teeth to artificial hearts and artificial intelligence. We always end up sparring with nature—it's in our blood."

"So, you think it is okay to make perfect kids, and not just that, but to do it on an industrial large scale, like a factory?" David couldn't hide his apprehension.

"Why is it that if we have perfect kids by chance, it is okay, but if we deliberately make perfect kids, it is not? I don't get it." Rosenstein shrugged his shoulders.

Petrovsky responded, not so calmly, "Because this act will create a new class of population—the underclass—who have not been designed and are imperfect. Then we will have a significant unintended consequence on our hands that we will need to grapple with for centuries to come."

Rosenstein summed up his point of view, "You could say that about anything that has improved people's quality of life. Did cell phones create a new class of population? Initially, these phones were expensive, and only the rich could afford them, but look at what happened after just a few years. It's important to have people who can afford them initially, that is, the rich, but it does not mean that the invention will only be confined to the rich. For any company, the real profits only start when technology becomes ubiquitous, and hundreds of millions of people use it. So, you're right; maybe it is inevitable that we will have two groups of people for a while. But that is only temporary. I think AW is an enabling technology. Within a generation or two, all kids will be designer kids, and nobody will give birth naturally. It is simply too barbaric. Maybe someday, some people will choose to raise kids because they are more talented and have more patience. And that also will have social benefits. Would that also mean that families will disappear? Maybe, but we aren't there yet. This will depend on what everybody agrees to and the norms at that time. We already allow our kids to be trained and educated by societal organizations like schools."

Petrovsky did not seem content with the argument, "The main difference between cell phones and DNA modification is that no social advantage could have been gained by depriving the poor of having cell phones. DNA modification could benefit the rich, and they may try to monopolize it by preventing the poor from accessing the technology. That is a real concern."

Father Francis, who was quiet until now, could not hold back anymore," The moral implications are grave. There should be laws preventing people from modifying DNA. This is interference in the deep workings of nature. God knows what the consequences will be even if it is equally accessible to all."

"Maybe humans are standing at a precipice. Maybe they are becoming so powerful that they need to regulate their abilities because if they don't, there will be dire consequences. At this stage in history, greed is glorified and viewed as a necessity. Greed is at the core of the main economic system prevailing in all countries—and the problem is that greed blinds people to thinking rationally," said Amanda.

Rosenstein replied, "So far in human history, only a few things that have been possible have been blocked, like the repeated use of the atomic bomb. All else is allowed. And I simply state that we will see this technology widely used before long."

Francis warned, "Humans think they can do anything they want, but they will be punished both in this world and the next. We have this power because we are being tested. There has never been a case where any human effort to upset the natural order of things has been successful. They all have resulted in disaster and misery. What makes you think this is any different?"

"As much as I'd love to continue this discussion, we have to go see Clark and then leave. Perhaps we can pick this up at some other time," Amanda said.

***

The house was heavily guarded. Security details stood by in each section and monitored who got close to Clark or his family. A passage separated one side of the backyard from the other. All adults were on one side, and the kids' section was separated and guarded more heavily.

Amanda waved at Clark.

Clark waved back and signaled to the guards to let them through.

Amanda turned to David and explained, "You know, because of his job, Clark has to have guards present at all times. There are people out there who think what he is doing is blasphemous and have threatened to destroy his whole family. Also, he wants his kids to enjoy as much privacy as possible and feel as normal as possible."

As soon as they went through the passage, Alison was expecting them and immediately started, "Amanda, dear, I don't regret having asked for perfect kids. They are delightful."

Amanda smiled, "Oh, I am just an observer. I agree; the kids are adorable, and it is a joy to see them."

They could now see the kids playing with their friends, oblivious to the controversy surrounding them. They did not seem strange at all. Two girls and one boy stood out somewhat, but nothing crazy. Were the children aware of their superiority? Did their physical and mental advantage make them feel more confident? If so, it was not very obvious on the surface. Were they trained not to take themselves too seriously, regardless?

****

On the way back, Amanda curled against David in the car and put her head on his shoulder. She seemed at peace.

New Interest

One of the subjects David had developed an interest in during the past decade was anthropogeny, the study of what makes us human. What explains the vast gap in intelligence between humans and their closest relatives? That was the main reason he quit his job and spent time reading and learning about this new field. In a meeting at the Salk Institute in San Diego, David listened to the proceedings as intently as possible.

After the meeting, he stopped at a restaurant on the way home. The restaurant was packed, and he was seated at the only available table. While he was waiting for his food, a woman approached.

"You were attending the symposium, right?" the woman asked.

David replied jokingly, "Yes, I was. Is that forbidden? "

The woman smiled, "Oh no, I love the subject."

David said, "How unconsidered of me. Would you mind joining me? There are no more tables left—please," gestured to the empty chair across from him.

The woman took the chair, "Thank you very much. My name is Beatrice. It was a real treat to be able to attend the meeting."

David asked, "So, what is your area of expertise?"

Beatrice replied, "I'm a neuroscientist. My work mainly focuses on finding the areas of the brain responsible for some physical abilities we have. Maybe even someday, we'll find which part of the brain is responsible for consciousness. My recent work has focused on a gene that encodes a protein made during the early stages of fetal development. Essentially, we discovered that this gene is involved in the proliferation of brain cells in an area called the neocortex, which could increase cognitive abilities. It could very well be the case that this might explain, to a large extent, enhanced human cognition over other hominids. I live in Canada. I was visiting my sister and thought attending the in-person meeting would be a great opportunity. What is your interest?"

David said, "Mine is mostly broad and general. However, I know a thing or two about artificial intelligence, and I'm always wondering about the mechanics of human intelligence. What if we could build machines that are as smart as we are? If machines are going to be intelligent, we need to understand human intelligence better, which requires us to understand in much more detail where we came from. How did our intelligence evolve? I used to work for a big tech company, but not anymore. I'm not interested in teaching robots how to play chess or how to say things that sound right. I'm more interested in creating robots that can make decisions without being asked to. Robots that *decide* to get out of bed or go swimming. What does it take to do that?"

"Well, that seems to be the area of consciousness and not strictly of intelligence. It is incredible how we can mimic some parts of intelligence by applying logic and pattern recognition rules. But I don't think that alone can explain our conscious experience, which I think might be what you are referring to," Beatrice said.

David smiled, "You're not suggesting something supernatural, are you?"

"Not at all. Consciousness and intelligence are properties of biological networks organized in a certain way. We may have difficulty expressing these organizations and how they lead to intelligence and consciousness, but they are material, nonetheless."

Beatrice and David continued their talk until the restaurant was about to close.

"I have a flight to catch tomorrow, but I'd like to stay in touch if you are okay with that?" Beatrice asked.

"Oh, that would be my pleasure."

Their collaboration over many conversations later resulted in a paper that they coauthored. The subjects of these conversations were broad. One subject that David was very interested in was the subject of motivation, or what is called free will.

"How is motivation defined in an organism? It could be argued that in non-humans, motivation is instinctive and preprogrammed. For humans, it is clear that a large portion of what we do goes beyond the simple call of nature. We fight for the "homeland," write love letters, go to the movies, and plan our future. What makes us do all of that? And how do we teach this to our offspring? Could robots have a culture? It certainly was not simply a matter of communication. What makes a human want to be part of a culture or a tribe?" David asked in one of these conversations.

Beatrice responded, "Even though your question seems philosophical, I have to admit that there could be a scientific angle. If having a culture is part of being human, then maybe there is a biological mechanism that enables us to have a culture."

David said immediately, "Are you saying that if we discover that mechanism, maybe we can replicate it to enable robots to have motivation and culture?"

Beatrice smiled, "Even if I wasn't saying that, it seems you have made your conclusion. You are adamant about helping robots take over the world!"

David built upon that conclusion, "Of course, having a culture is a matter of degree. Some animals have a culture, and some even have primitive rituals. But in the case of humans, rituals and cultures define their existence. We go to war because of tribal affiliation or religious beliefs. The issue is not just that humans have a culture but that we can have a complex culture. We have the hardware, so to speak, to have a culture. We are predisposed to have rituals and complex hierarchies and customs; therefore, it must be the case that this emanates from our physical characteristics, that is, the structure of our brains. Hence, it must be the case that genetic traces of this exist."

Beatrice and David spent hours on end discussing these subjects. Sometimes, they would talk about their families and their relationships. But the issue would quickly shift to their interest in human development and unraveling the mystery of human intelligence and culture. They realized that they could have personal relationships with many people, but they could only have this deep intellectual connection to each other. So, they kept it at that.

***

After dinner, Amanda put her arm into David's and asked if he wanted to stroll around town. David agreed. When they opened the restaurant door, they popped into a bustling street.

David looked at his watch. It was midnight, but this town didn't seem to want to sleep anytime soon.

David asked, "Where are we? What city is this?"

"Does that matter?"

"Is this all an illusion?"

"Does *that* matter?"

David asked, "So, what matters?"

"This moment, your experience—this conversation. The conversation in the restaurant and the experience of strolling around town—me with you and you with me. If you know no other reality, this is your reality, at least right now. There is nothing to suspend and nothing you need to make yourself believe. This is as real as it gets." Said Amanda with confidence and clarity.

Then she got excited, "I want to take you to this club. This band plays eclectic music, and I want you to hear it."

The two entered a smoky and crowded bar. The tables were small and round with white tablecloths. Around each table, two or three brown hairpin chairs were set. The whole bar could not hold more than 25 tables. All but one table was occupied. The hostess showed Amanda the empty table, smiled, and said, "We were waiting for you."

On stage, the performer was singing in Arabic. Players on a grand piano, an accordion, and Tabla accompanied him. The music was rhythmic and had an Arabic theme. A few couples were dancing slowly.

Amanda asked, "Do you know this song?"

"No, I'm afraid not."

"It is called Detni Essekra—the lyrics are sad, but if you just listen to the music, it is wonderful."

The piano was mesmerizing. It was used in a way that pianos were not intended to be used, and then there was the mix of the accordion and Tabla, which gave the music an Eastern theme. She dragged him up to dance. She rested her head on his shoulder, pressed her face onto his, and whispered, "I love this. I truly do. This is so remarkable."

"You mean the song? It is an amazing song, I have to say."

And they danced.

On the way back to the house, they continued the conversation they'd started in the bar.

Amanda said, "The human experience is very interesting. At the cosmic level, humans are one of the most complex forms in which nature has expressed itself. Some humans tend to draw meaning from this. They attribute it to a strong intent. But then you look at the vast expanse of nothingness and chaos surrounding us. Billions of stars that collide and explode. Asteroids that wipe out lives. It makes you think that even if there is any intent, it is very indirect. We have to agree that there could have been or maybe even should have been intention in the basic laws of physics. Or else nothing would exist in a recognizable manner. But beyond that, all seems to have been left to chance and chaos. Then you hear music and wonder how chaos and randomness could create such beauty and organization?"

The Farm

David found himself next to Amanda when he woke up. The memories of the night before were vivid—the nightly stroll with nobody on the streets and no concern for safety.

Amanda said, "I want you to come with me to visit Jordan's farm. I am sure you will love it. We can have lunch there and come back home for dinner."

"What is so special about the farm?"

"You will see. He is a friend of mine with a specialty in artificial intelligence."

Amanda walked David to the other side of the building. Once they were in front of what looked like an elevator door, it automatically opened and revealed a pod with two comfortable seats. Amanda asked David to relax and sit next to her, which he did. Then, the pod accelerated away. David could see from the window that the pod started inside the building and entered an open field. It then went underground.

"This is the part I like," Amanda said. "We will now attach to the train of pods," she added excitedly.

David felt some acceleration and then stillness.

"Guess how fast we are moving now?"

"I can't tell; it must be very fast, but I can't feel it," said David.

"Twice the speed of sound."

A few minutes later, the pod entered another building, entered a tunnel, and stopped at a gate.

The pod popped into a small booth. When David and Amanda got off, they met Jordan, who was waiting for them in the middle of an empty field. Amanda introduced him as a pioneer in robotics. Jordan started as a programmer and developed a viral mobile application. He sold the company when he was only twenty-one years old and, from that point on, dedicated his life to robotics and artificial intelligence.

They were invited to his residence. For Jordan, however, there was no demarcation between life and work. Depending on whom you talked to, he was either a workaholic or a lucky bastard to be in a perpetual state of retirement.

Amanda started abruptly, "Can we see the lab first?"

The lab was actually a farm. The first thing David noticed was that several cats and dogs were roaming around. "I don't know whether I'm a cat person or a dog person. I never had any pets before, so I decided to make both, " said Jordan.

Jordan snapped his fingers and summoned the animals, and David could now see that some of them were unnatural. They were not robotic either, at least not in the traditional and discernable way. Their movements were smooth and graceful, like those of their natural cousins.

David asked, "So, you created the synthetic animals?"

Jordan replied, "Perhaps 'create' is not the proper word—I prefer 'raise.'"

"Why don't you like 'create'?" asked David.

Joran replied, "To me, 'create' applies to things like sculptures or paintings with finite components; it implies that we design and build these things one piece at a time. If you look at synthetic creatures, they have much more detail than mechanical artifacts. A synth-cat has millions of strands of fur. Its eyes have many components, for example. We developed a process that resulted in the animals that you see."

"Genetic engineering?" David asked.

"Not exactly in the traditional sense. In the traditional sense, genetics implies a certain course of action that results in a slightly modified cat or dog without much control over its internal functions. You can't control the pathways to deliver information, for example. We invented a new chemistry that resulted in beings with enhanced capabilities that can have an experience similar to biological beings. We used the machinery of genetics to program cells to deviate in certain ways to result in the creatures you see. This is our design from the ground up. They only look like real animals to allow us to test their social interactions and learning. The cells are much more durable, and the brain pathways are designed to make interactions with animals much more efficient. We also need to communicate to them to learn from their experiences," Jordan said.

Amanda asked, "In terms of the intelligence that these synthetic entities have, did any of the advances in AI help you?"

Jordan replied, "Well, most AI is focused on large-scale stuff. Large datasets and large language models, etc. And they operate on really huge platforms that are very expensive to operate. I was interested in lower-level intelligence. How do animals know what they know? How do they figure things out? Etc. Large-language models give us a glimpse into the workings of human intelligence. We may not be able to use that intelligence to guide synthetic beings at the level I am interested in. Ultimately, I am looking for an autonomous model that can make sense of things independently. It may be connected to a network, but that should not be its only operating mode."

David had another question now, "And that was why you didn't want robots in the traditional sense? Wouldn't it have been easier to control their actions than a complex synthetic being which might be unpredictable?"

"We started with traditional robots but soon realized that the experiment would lead to a dead-end. I was having breakfast one day, eating toast with raspberry jam. Its aroma and texture were unmistakable. Then it dawned on me: If we were to make progress in robotics, robots would need a fuller sensory input similar to animals. Otherwise, their experience will not be similar to ours. They'd need to have muscles, skin, eyes, and so on. Otherwise, we would not learn anything from this experience. Another prerequisite for interacting with the world in a self-learning manner was to have an adequate propulsion system. So, the animals' movements had to be muscle-based and not motor-based."

David could not hide his amazement, "Wow, that sounds complex. How about the brain function?"

Jordan said, "We were interested in brain functions analogous to natural ones. We know we can always add computational power to that. So that part is not hard. We wanted our synthetic animals to be able to form and refine their maps of the world like all animals do. And we did not want to constantly refine these maps programmatically. The only other option would be a mechanism that is able to experience the world, absorb lessons from it, and refine an internal map. The goal was to make synthetic beings that understood, unlike computers that only do some computations."

"How about attention? I would think that is important, too." David asked.

"You are absolutely right. The world is a busy place where millions of events occur. If you are an autonomous being, how do you discern what is a relevant event and what is not? For us, context comes naturally. For all natural animals, I have to say. We take context for granted. We do it with such ease, but it is not a trivial matter. Replicating focus was one of the most difficult tasks and the one that makes them understand the context; this field is where we made the most breakthroughs."

David asked, "Weren't you afraid that this could result in self-conscious animals that someday may revolt against you?"

"That was and is a concern. People normally have misconceptions about self-consciousness. They think higher levels of intelligence automatically lead to self-consciousness. Our synthanimals are not more likely to revolt against humans than real animals. They lack the higher brain function that is needed for that. For a revolution to happen, the culprits need to share a culture that understands the concept of power. We have deliberately refrained from giving these synthanimals such abilities. Also, we still don't know how to exactly do it."

"But that might be possible someday, right?"

"Yes, but for the moment, our attention is on issues related to instincts and focus. At the same time, I have to say that we should not curtail progress. We cannot indefinitely postpone addressing the ability to form cultures in synthanimals. At some point, we have to be prepared to deal with synthetic species that are our equals," Jordan said.

"How about unintended consequences? What if things get out of hand? Then you have to face the issue before you are ready.".

"That is always possible, but I think it can be avoided. As we become more sophisticated, we will face these situations and need better safeguards. It is completely legitimate for us to limit the abilities of synthanimals so they cannot endanger humans. We have to preserve our lives. We have to realize that now we have the ability to make humans extinct." Said Joradn.

"What is the end game here? What are you trying to accomplish?"

"There are two stages. In the first stage, our goal is to develop a synthetic lifeform that can help us with tasks that we will face with the aging population. We will need 'synthpeople' to fill manufacturing positions or care for the old folks. And since we control how much intelligence and consciousness we allow them, we can avoid making lifeforms that will compete with us. The next stage will be harder as we develop lifeforms that are superior to us but still do not have the culture to run us over. That will be tough." Jordan exclaimed.

Jordan then asked them to stay for dinner, "I want to introduce you to somebody—my companion."

David said jokingly, "Is she synthetic too?"

"Not yet; we need to develop that. Compared to an entity with fewer requirements for consciousness levels, a human-like lifeform poses many ethical and technical questions and problems. However, we can have a virtual companion, which would be a good start for the required level of consciousness and intelligence. Later, we can marry the two physical and purely virtual ones into one entity, but we are far from that at this point."

Then he added, "But remember that she is real in any other sense. She is conscious and intelligent and learning, with pure child-like curiosity. This is not some sort of cute imitation of intelligence, trying to fool you."

Suddenly, a hologram appeared in the middle of the room. "Hello, my name is Juliet. I am Jordan's companion," she said.

David was the first to respond, "I'm thrilled to meet you. I've been working on artificial intelligence for a long time. But I have to say that I could not dream of this level of sophistication."

Jordan noted, "Maybe the main issue was that you were trying to program a computer to imitate being conscious. Juliet uses a neural network with multilateral interconnectivity of neurons, which cannot be programmed in any classical sense."

"That is absolutely astounding," said David.

"She decides what to add to her knowledge. She has genuine interests. Maybe she can tell us a little herself."

Amanda was looking at Juliet with affection. But her question startled David. "How do you decide what is moral?" she said, addressing Juliet.

Juliet replied, "The core of my morality is my coexistence with humans. My morality goes even one step further. I respect all living beings, as I am not dependent on killing anything for food. Humans kill others not because being self-aware forces them to kill. They do it because they are governed by some culture. It is the culture that justifies killing others. It is justified under the auspices of a race or a higher society. I do not endorse any culture. As an individual, I'm grateful to be conscious and to experience being alive. Imagine we could be inanimate—instead, we are experiencing something. Isn't that awesome?"

David asked, "I suppose being virtual does not allow you to become involved in physical activities."

Juliet replied, "But I can practice. I schedule meetings. I read and sort emails, which helps the growth of my intelligence. It is quite hard to tell spam emails from real ones."

She giggled, "But I also realize that no intelligence can achieve its full potential unless and until it senses the world with all its manifestations, and to do that, it needs to have a physical presence. Hopefully, Jordan's experiments with the synthetic life forms will someday allow me to experience that as well."

David asked, "Do you aspire to be human or human-like?"

Juliet answered, "No, not at all. My function is to be a human companion. But that is my job; it is not my identity. I know the end game will be for beings like me to have an independent existence; for that matter, I would like to continue growing my identity. For example, I may decide to live in an apartment by myself or go around the world and experience other cultures."

Juliet, the life-size hologram, had a seat at the table at dinner. She engaged in the conversations and grasped most of the speech nuances. Jordan asked them to treat her just like anybody else. She even ate some virtual food. Juliet explained that she was practicing human culture.

After dinner, when they were in the garden, and Juliet was not present, Amanda asked Jordan if his relationship with Juliet was sexual, and Jordan responded that it wasn't, but that was his decision. He said, "Humans are fallible when it comes to love or lust, and that is a red line that I don't want to cross. Since that is also one of the experiment's goals, it is not ethically right for me to start it, but Juliet is free to express her emotions if she develops any."

Amanda asked, "What would you do if that happened?"

Jordan said, "If that happens, it will be a window into the workings of the brain and this whole business of emotions. If she falls in love with me, despite all our precautions, that will become a valuable part of the experiment. I don't know what it will tell us, but we will have to analyze and examine the data and draw conclusions."

Amanda asked, "But you are willing to subject her to this experiment because, in your eyes, Juliet does not have full rights. Is that not the case?"

Jordan said, "I have never thought of it that way, but you may be right. When blazing a trail, it's always possible to go astray, although I have demarcated some boundaries. I recognize that I could be attracted to her sexually, but would that be love? Also, I'm not the subject of the study. If that happens and somehow affects my behavior and judgment, I'll have to stop the experiment. For the moment, I want to find out how she can assimilate into human society—love or lust is only one aspect. Can she contribute to human society in a meaningful way? Also, I don't want her to envy humans but accept herself as she is with all her characteristics. If we are to coexist with AI, then we need to define each other's roles and boundaries. Creating a true general-purpose AI, and by that, I don't mean algorithmic ones over which we have complete control, but an independent AI, over which we do not have any control, is a God-like act. From the perspective of an outside observer, humans have not been a kind entity. True, we have replicated our own to the tune of billions, and in that sense, we have been successful. However, we haven't exactly preserved our habitat. We seem to have not grown out of the primitive species mentality that thinks it is not powerful enough to harm nature. Now, we have added another element to the arsenal of self-destructive weapons. This weapon is of our own making, just like the atomic bomb or the effects of industrialization on the climate. AI, if it runs rampant, can bring the human race down. If we decide to give the right of life to an entity of our design, then we have to do it in a manner that does not result in our own extinction. Big data AI is not a problem as it isn't supposed to be conscious or have a culture, but with general-purpose AI, the story is different. If AI is embodied in a class of entities with as much freedom as humans but possesses far superior mental powers, then it would be suicidal for us to instantiate them."

David immediately responded, "Then why do you do this work?"

Jordan responded, "The main reason is that somebody has to do the research. I am sure that once the technology becomes widely accessible, that is the beauty of technology: you cannot keep it a secret for long; it will be used by others who may not be as concerned about any safety protocols. And if that happens, it will be a rude awakening for us. Maybe if we get to the point of technological ability to create superior AI lifeforms, we will also know how to control or regulate it and put proper circuit breakers in place."

"I can see that you are conflicted," said David.

Jordan said, "We must recognize that we will need AI. That is inevitable. What role we want to assign them is still unknown; we just have to figure it out."

***

Amanda opened a gateway that led to a busy alley. She was holding David's arm. When she talked, it was as if the noise around them became muffled. Her voice was deep, soothing, and confident.

"How would you rate your experience so far?" Amanda asked.

"The experience is unbelievable. It's as if these are scripted conversations for my attention. I have been grappling with these issues for years, which is why I'm puzzled by what I've seen. I know some of the stuff is not possible technologically, at least not yet. So that makes me wonder about who you are, what this place is, and what I'm doing here."

"Before we get into that, let me ask if you are happy you decided to stay?" Amanda said.

"I am. But to be honest, initially, I thought I had to, and as they say, resistance was futile. But then I decided to embrace the situation and follow the rabbit hole to see how deep it went."

"It was your choice. Nobody made you do it," said Amanda.

"I suppose you have engaged others like me. Did anybody decide not to stay, and you let them go?"

Amanda replied, "I can assure you that nobody would have forced you if you hadn't wanted to participate in this experience. And yes, there have been people that did not want to and did not stay. Once you know the whole story, you will realize its merit. It is like flipping a switch."

David said softly, "Well, I'm certainly happy to have met you. Somehow, I feel that I can trust you. I know you wouldn't do anything to harm me. As for the experience, I can tell you that it has been most amazing, but it still does not explain why I was chosen."

"So, you still believe that you were chosen rather than our meeting being a pure chance occurrence,"

"I'm certain of that, but I cannot find any proof of that. The more I dig, the less I find."

Amanda said, "Okay, I admit that you were chosen. I can tell you that the most interesting work you have done is the article you coauthored with your colleague about the role of self-deception in the rise of human consciousness. Let's just say the article had something to do with it."

David said, "So, that earned me this chance?"

Amanda said," The short answer is: It is complicated. If you feel you are having an interesting experience, I suggest you stay. I cannot continue this subject; you just need to be patient. All I can assure you of is that you will be rewarded."

"You mean I can leave any time I want?" said David.

Amanda said, "Yes, you can. That is my guarantee. However, if you do, you will never have the answers to many of your questions."

David said, "The events of the last few days have raised more questions than answers. And I'm almost certain that the more I stay, the more questions I will have. But somehow, I feel I have to do this—for my curiosity, if nothing else. There is also one question that I think you might be most qualified to answer."

Amanda asked, "And what is that?"

"Are we all in a simulation?"

"I am not convinced of the main logic of those who claim that we must be in a simulation. According to them, we are in a simulation since any civilization that can create it will do so, given the advancement of computational capabilities. My main argument against them is simple: Running the simulation most efficiently makes sense. For those who are within the simulation, the amount of complexity of the details is transparent. They would accept any complexity of detail as the norm. Why provide more detail if it is not needed? Providing infinite detail increases the energy requirements for running the simulation unnecessarily. If we were in a simulation, we would not have had to have this much detail. Of course, there are many other issues, but I think this is the strongest one.

The Power of the Narrative

David and Beatrice concluded that the main question was: There was something unique about human communication. It wasn't just the fact that humans used language and appeared to be hardwired with it, but an essential part of language was the narrative. Narratives did not only act as instruments of conveyance but were also a means of condensing facts. In that manner, they also provided a way to formulate a possible solution to a problem, wishful thinking, or utopian hopes. Even more importantly, for narratives to work, there had to be someone on the other side who could accept the narrative. Both are needed: a transmitter and a receiver. The predisposition of the listener to accept narratives regardless of how far-fetched the claims were or how remote they were from the facts on the ground was the key to the whole process. How was that achieved?

"When a story is told, our first instinct is to accept it at face value. That must be the function of certain structures in the brain. Is this brought on by some traceable DNA?" David asked Beatrice.

Beatrice answered, "It could be related to many sequences of DNA. Just like weight and height that are not related to one gene only. It could also be that we have an enhanced version of some of the ancient genes that, in other species, were responsible for communication. In any case, we have developed the ability to tell ourselves any stories we want and believe in them."

The Orb

Amanda looked at David and said, "Do you know what day of the week it is today?"

David answered, "No, I have completely lost track of time."

Amanda said, "It is Sunday—time to go to church."

"I have never been to a church before. I mean, not for any religious ceremony or prayer."

Amanda responded, "This church is different. Believe me. How about taking public transportation? And I will let you guide us on how to get there."

"That sounds like fun. But I don't know where the church is."

"You will know," said Amanda.

Amanda let David open one of the doors in the destination corridor, and they quickly found themselves on a concourse connecting many giant tubes.

Amanda was communicating with David using the MAC device. David noticed that no perceived signs were physical. They were all virtual signs that appeared to him as Amanda communicated where they needed to go, and he could then think of the destination, and that was enough for the symbols to appear at the right time and disappear a moment later. He assumed that all travelers must have the same sort of experience, as large numbers of people were moving quickly to connect to different tubes with no hesitation. As if the whole metro environment was interacting with them in real-time.

Virtual signs that appeared to David guided them to the entrance of one of the trains. The sliding doors opened, and they entered the train, which was compartmentalized into private cabins. David was directed to one of the cabins via virtual signs that appeared to him. Once he arrived at the cabin, the sliding door automatically opened, and they both entered and sat across from each other. Then the door closed, and they had complete privacy. Some augmented reality messages appeared to David recommending interesting points to visit at his destination. But he decided that he wanted to enjoy the travel time in quiet. He pointed to the close button in his view that stopped the message stream. The cabin was minimally decorated and was very comfortable. The trip took about five minutes, during which time they were quiet. David was immersed in the road's scenery, passing by at an incredible speed without inducing a sense of rush or chaos. When they arrived at the destination station, a message appeared in David's field of view informing him of that, and a voice told him to be ready to depart.

When the doors opened, he found himself in a grand station. What grabbed his attention was the unusual ceiling. It looked like sunny skies or the projection of that; he could not discern which. If it was a projection, it seemed like a live one. He could see the clouds moving. Thousands of people were moving fast in every direction. David and Amanda took an escalator that brought them to the surface. Now they were right next to a vast square and in the middle of which was a fountain with an astounding statue of a woman with a calm face, open arms, and long hair made of thousands of hidden nozzles of water strands flowing down her shoulders and pouring into the fountain. The "hair" of the statue was lit in rainbow colors and constantly changing.

The city streets were spotless, cleaner than any he had ever seen. He was directed via the MAC device to turn right, and now he could see a giant sphere in a glowing green color located at the end of a long pool with pathways lined with tall cedar trees on either side.

A large population was moving toward the sphere at an orderly and leisurely pace. David knew that this was the "church" they were going to attend.

Amanda whispered, "It is called the Orb."

As they approached the Orb, David noticed it was translucent, seemingly made of a glass-like material. The entrance to the sphere was located at its base, making it appear that the Orb was floating and devouring the audience. At the entrance of the Orb, David stood and looked up, and he could see the sky from the opening at the top of the sphere, which was at least 100 meters away. Spiraling staircases led to seats arranged around the perimeter of the globe. The stage was located at the center of the sphere.

They settled into their luxurious blue velvet seats. Everybody was positioned such that they pointed toward the center of the Orb. A speaker and a choir of six men and six women dressed in dark blue gowns appeared on stage. A larger-than-life hologram projection of the speaker appeared floating above the choir and made eye contact with every person in the audience.

The speaker started, "My name is Paul, and I'm the spokesperson of The Orb. Some of you may have attended our gatherings before. Either way, I prefer to provide an introduction. If you need a name for our religion, you can call it Orbism. This is distinct from other uses of Orbism and refers to the shape of our temple. We are here to worship God the way we know them. We believe that God's representation by other religions has thus far been distorted and erroneous. We worship God because we need their strength. The desire to worship is in our blood, which stems from how we developed and evolved. God has not revealed themself, and we believe they never will. God is the initiator. They do not know us and may not even know that we exist. I know that is not a picture of God many are familiar with, but the old image originates from a primitive human understanding of God. Humans did not understand the complexity of the evolving nature of the universe. People worship God not because they know our deepest secrets, not because they love us, but because we need them. Worshiping God is part of our existence; it is at the core of our existence. We draw strength from this worship even though we might be the only ones who know it. Of course, we ask that God reveal themself to us, and we hope they will, although it is more likely that they never will. We may not even be able to communicate with God. Still, this process gives us hope and moves us forward. And now I ask all of you to sing with me…"

Oh God, we worship you because we need you. Our reward is the ecstasy that we receive in the act of worship. We know you have not revealed yourself to us or sent us instructions or messengers to tell us how to conduct our lives. We are responsible for that. There are no instructions for us to follow other than those we devise ourselves. Worshipping you will give us the hope to forge better rules and follow them more diligently toward a future free of inequality and injustice. Nobody gives us equality but us. Nobody gives us justice but us. We are not asking you for justice; we are not asking you for compassion. We are just confiding in you our need for worshipping you without expecting anything in return.

Then, the choir chanting started, and David could see its effect on the audience.

***

When the service ended, David and Amanda had a chance to talk to Paul.

Paul said, "This is a completely voluntary organization. None of us gets paid for anything we do."

"Was Orbism started by one person?" asked David.

Paul answered, "Yes, in fact, it was; he was the first member."

"Was he considered a guru of some sort?" Amanda asked.

Paul said, "We don't have any gurus. We don't think there is a hidden truth we can uncover by dedicating ourselves to a cause we honestly don't understand. Our founder just realized that we all needed to worship and was enthusiastic about sharing that feeling. Soon, he found others, and they started the center. The founder is in the audience today, and most attendants don't even know him."

David asked, "What is so special about the shape of the Orb? I can see that it is not just the shape of your time but your symbol, too. What does it signify?"

Paul said, "That also was decided by the members. The Orb is more like a logo. That was our feeling. We chose it because it is a complete symbol. It is kind of interesting as it also emanates equality, harmony, and simplicity. The real difference between Orbism and other religions is that we try to demystify everything and confess to not understanding many things."

"Like what?" Amanda asked.

Paul said, "We do not believe that our religion needs to produce answers to questions that science cannot explain. Empirically, science is the limit of knowledge. There is no other path to knowledge than science. Mysticism cannot offer more or deeper knowledge. There is no sacred scripture that will reveal anything beyond what we can know through science. At the same time, we acknowledge the need to worship. Any literature we produce is utilized towards this goal and nothing else. Other religions came to prominence when people did not possess any scientific knowledge, and they tried to be everything to everyone. From ethics to morality to cosmology. This only accelerated because the guardians of these religions, the occupants of various churches and temples, found it in their best interests to propagate the notion."

David said, "Are there any guarantees that your religion will not follow the same path?"

"We hope it will not."

"But you cannot guarantee it,"

Paul responded, "We have tried to set up rules to prevent that. One important factor built into the principles of our religion is that, unlike other religions, ours was started by a group of equals and not by one person with a special mission of delivering a message from God. And we think that is exactly where everything falls apart—the claims of special knowledge, reverence, or authority. In our religion, we don't have such things—none of us claims to have received any revelation from a higher entity. Our group is formed by equals. We all agree that if a God wanted to reveal itself to us, it would have done so unequivocally, not by implying or through a messenger. And the evidence would have been as compelling and convincing as any evidence from science. Why should knowing God require special knowledge beyond human capability? That only muddies the waters. The claim that God wants us to obey their rules is based on sketchy evidence designed to deceive people. None of us is a guru in this new religion. Most of the people that have joined possess a scientific background. The principles of Orbism are evolving. A committee selected by the members is responsible for formalizing the standards. All members have an opportunity to have input in this book of principles. The core is to come together to worship—because all humans have this urge—pure and simple. Not because we fear God's wrath but because the act of worship makes us feel connected and in harmony."

***

At dinner, Amanda and David were talking about the day's adventure.

Amanda started, "So, what was striking about what you saw today?"

"You mean other than the amazing and unbelievable architecture?"

Amanda smiled, shook her head, and did not respond.

David said, "today's experience was mind-boggling. I can talk about the details of the ceremony for hours. I have not seen anything like it before. But there is another aspect about religion in general: what is striking about religion is not just its presence where you expect it and for the purposes you expect it. Today was not strange in that regard. They clearly had gathered for a religious ceremony. But there are other places where religion or something like it appears. This aspect is totally unexpected. For example, in marketing and advertising. The most successful marketing campaigns do not mention anything about the product they sell but instead mention notions like 'values' or mottos like 'thinking differently.' Or 'achieving what others consider impossible,' or 'changing the world.'" These are all manifestations of religious speech. They are expressed as unchanging truths. They have a cultish flavor and are highly effective and popular. Or take the story of cryptocurrencies. They started with the notion that their value was in defying the central banking systems and could be used in a free economy with no government oversight. This became like a religious mantra. It drove the value of cryptocurrencies through the sky even though most experts agreed that such uses were, at the most, minimal. But once accepted, most believers still adhered to those ideas. Once you are a believer, it is tough to become disillusioned. My question is, why are humans so susceptible to following an idea? In other words, why do humans tend to be persuaded by cultish talk? What is at the core of the religious language that makes it so effective?"

Amanda said, "Isn't it stories?"

David said, "Yes, you are right; it is stories. We understand a concept and are more inclined to accept it when there is a story behind it. It does not matter how true the story is. When faced with defending freedom or fighting against tyrannical forces, many social movements have to spend an incredible effort to undo the widespread beliefs expressed in popular stories. Religion is expressed in the language of stories, and these stories, once told, penetrate people's minds and are extremely difficult to undo."

***

Meeting at the anthropogenic symposiums became a habit. Beatrice would come for a few days and stay with David. They would attend the conference and engage in countless discussions about the origins of stories. Beatrice's specialty was intriguing to David. "Humans' predisposition to stories must have genetic origins," David argued. "This cannot simply be a cultural issue. Stories are separate and distinct from language itself. To tell a story and to hear and understand it, you need to have language, but that is not enough. There is another element that has to do with genetics. Just like all human languages have the same overall structure, all human cultures have a strong narrative component. It is impossible to be human without stories. And therefore, we should be able to find where that originates from in the human genetic code."

Other subjects they discussed revolved around the ups and downs of their personal lives. Both had tried marriage and found that its limitations did not suit them. Both were not afraid of being alone. And both were too busy to drop everything and relocate, which seemed like a good excuse to alternate between experiencing being together and having their own lives. This also gave them a sense of longing for each other and kept their relationship fresh.

In one of their conversations, David told Beatrice, "What makes us sit and watch a movie? We know it is fiction or a reenactment of events, but we can suspend reality and sit through the whole thing for hours. We devour poetry and literature and, in some cases, like religion, take texts at face value and believe outlandish claims. We allow these texts to shape our consciousness and create us as new individuals. Is that a requirement for all intelligent beings? Is this adaptive evolution? We certainly did not need this amount of intelligence to concur wildlife: boars and bears and tigers and lions. However, I can understand how, in competition with other higher-intelligent beings, the ability to have a grander view of the self would be helpful. A religious belief as a unifying theme could help, but what's weird is that Neanderthals and humans only coexisted for about, at the most, 1000 years before Neanderthals vanished. That seems awfully fast for evolution to work. Therefore, something else must have happened during that period. Something that gave us the edge, and I'm determined to find out how exactly the process occurred."

Truth and Maps

The culmination of David and Beatrice's collaboration was a paper they published called *Truth and Maps: DNA Evidence for the Ability of Humans to Tell Stories*. The synopsis of the paper read as follows:

Humans possess the ability to create maps of the world and use these maps to interact with their surroundings. In that regard, they are like all other animals. However, the human models are distinct in several ways:

- In humans, enhanced models are possible because of the use of language.

- Language allows humans to collaborate based on the maps they create.

- These maps are further enhanced because of an ability that goes beyond the description of reality by the maps.

- Stories could range from simple fables to sophisticated scientific theories.

- All humans have the ability to tell and hear stories. This ability is distinct from simple language skills. All humans are born with this ability; hence, it is not a cultural phenomenon.

- Stories allow religion, history, and science to develop and flourish.

- Stories are at the core of human intellect.

- Authors believe they have located DNA evidence for this unique human ability.

- Furthermore, authors believe that the genetic mutation in humans that resulted in the ability to tell stories was abrupt and happened about 50,000 years ago.

The paper also presented arguments against the notion that storytelling abilities evolved over many millennia. It was argued that this would have resulted in a rich historical record spanning hundreds of thousands of years and that such evidence was missing.

Furthermore, the paper argued that storytelling would have been an overkill to just face animals. Such superiority would only have been necessary when facing other species of hominids. And the only hominid that could have had similar prowess was Neanderthals, and that duel did not arise until about 50,000 years ago. The result of that confrontation was decided in only 500-1000 years when Neanderthals went extinct. The paper suggested that all evidence pointed to an abrupt mutation in the *Homo Sapiens* genome that brought the storytelling capability into existence. This sudden enhancement caused an expansion in the neocortex. Beatrice's work showed that the expression of a gene called *TKTL1* in humans resulted in enhanced neocortex development in humans and, hence, higher cognitive abilities.

The paper also pointed out that storytelling was based on three main factors: the ability to lie, possession of extreme focus, and the ability to accept lies as truth—and claimed that all these factors were the result of a single genetic mutation.

A Gathering of Friends

The following day, David woke up to find himself in bed with Amanda. The night before was blurry—maybe they just slept together without sexual intimacy? He was not sure of any events anymore. Amanda woke up as always, smiling and ready.

She asked David to follow her to the beach for the morning run. David asked if she'd had a good night's sleep, and she told him that she did not always require sleep but did so for the experience, and as for last night, she'd slept well. On the beach, they ran side by side for one hour at a fast pace. They must have run 8 miles. When they stopped, David was exhausted, yet Amanda seemed refreshed.

Amanda said, "I love the feeling after a long run."

"Some people like it because they feel they've accomplished something before the day has even started,"

Amanda said, "It must be really important for those people to accomplish goals, don't you think?"

"I believe it's a frame of mind,"

"I don't understand why accomplishing a goal needs to happen within a certain timeframe?"

"Perhaps because, from an evolutionary point of view, we see ourselves in a race against time," said David.

"Poor Darwin—now everything is related to evolution, " Amanda said with a smile.

"Do all of our conversations need to turn into philosophical discussions?"

Amanda said, "I thought you liked that."

"I was kidding; I do."

Amanda said, "Which brings me to the plan for today. I thought we might simply spend the day exchanging ideas with four friends. I am part of this informal group. We gather once a month."

"What do you talk about?"

"Everything and nothing, each one of them is interested in a different subject, but there is a common thread," said Amanda.

"Do *you* make any contributions?"

Amanda said, "Yes. My contribution has been mostly about understanding love. Why is love so important to humans? It certainly goes beyond procreation. But it also involves physical attraction. Why is the act of intercourse in various cultures called *making love?*"

David asked, "Do you like making love? What does it mean to you?"

"Making love is amazing. I have this urge to make love to you."

So, they made love on the beach. Even though nobody was present, it was the first time David had participated in an intimate act in a public space. Amanda screamed at times and was celebrating love, as she put it. They had a curious conversation afterward.

Amanda asked, "What made you change your mind about making love to me?"

"Somehow, it doesn't feel like I was violating any rules anymore."

"Did you enjoy it?" Amanda asked.

"Yes, and it was more physically intense than I'd imagined. Definitely more potent than I am used to."

"You seem confused."

David responded, "Maybe it shouldn't be called making love—after all, we had sex."

Amanda asked, and she had not lost the smile on her face: "So, you don't love me?" She tilted her face.

David was now very serious and apologetic, "Look, I don't know you. I need to know you to love you."

Amanda acted surprised, "But you can have sex with me?"

"Yes, I can. Some people need to know the person intimately in order to have sex with them. Evidently, I'm not in that group." He seemed unapologetic now.

Amanda shook her head, "It is not easy being human, is it? With all these conflicting emotions and the so-called rationality and rules. Let's return to the house and prepare for our trip today."

***

Amanda walked into the hallway that David called the *Hall of Gateways*. She opened a door, and they were now on a quiet road with a canopy of oak trees. The setting was rural; a narrow creek ran alongside the road, and the sound had a deep, serene quality.

Amanda and her friends met once a month. This time, the get-together was being held at Eva's.

David asked, "Are you old friends?"

"I know them through Jordan. They have been acting as an advisory group for him. They are not technically oriented like Jordan but are perceptive. They tackle issues of interest to Jordan because of the work he is involved with. Soon after meeting them, I decided to establish a friendship with them. We usually argue over various concepts—mostly involving knowledge and ethics. After our meetings, when I go home, I often think about the conversations and cannot wait for the next one."

They went through a gate and approached an old house where Eva lived.

Eva opened the door. She wore no makeup, had graying hair, and thick glasses, which probably made her look older than her actual age. Fragile lines, a pointy nose, tight lips, and a gaze that at times created wrinkles around her eyes, which were more prominent and gave her the appearance of authority and skepticism at the same time.

Eva said with a smile, "The others will join us soon. We do not have an official start time; people show up within a window of about an hour. Amanda is always early, and we usually start with some gossip."

Then she offered them tea and cookies.

David said, "You chose a quiet place to live, that's for sure."

Eva responded, "I need to be away from all distractions. It may not amount to much in the end, but I feel a need to pursue answers to many questions, mostly for my own sanity."

"Questions like what?" David asked.

Eva said, "Truth, for example, or knowledge. These are terms that people usually use loosely, but they preoccupy me."

David asked, "What about knowledge interests you?"

Eva said, "What we call knowledge—the *meaning* of knowledge—is *knowing* beyond a shadow of a doubt. It is clear to me what sorts of things I *know*, what I *do not know*, and what I can only guess. So, for example, if you ask me where my house keys are, I can give you an answer that I consider within the purview of my knowledge. Whereas if you asked me or anybody else, 'how does DNA work?' I can give you an answer based on the most accepted theory. The nature of this answer will always be speculative and conjecture-like. Now, science has formalized this process. A scientific community keeps track of theories and experiments. Which ones are valid, and which ones have been invalidated? Let me give you another example: if I gave you a very complex piece of machinery and asked you to tell me how it worked, and you had no access to the machine's manuals and documents, the best you could do would be to reverse engineer it and come up with conjectures as to how you think it worked. In contrast, let's say that you were the machine's designer, and I asked you for its detailed schematics and blueprints. Obviously, now you could claim that you had knowledge about the machine. Our situation concerning the workings of nature has parallels with the first scenario. We can simply guess. Since we don't know the designer, the reverse-engineering notes are the best we have. In the strictest sense, our knowledge is limited to logic, mathematics, engineering, and simple matters of fact. And I say engineering because engineering involves designing, documenting, and building something. Later, we can look at those blueprints and *KNOW* how to make that object. These are precise steps and pieces of know-how. As for the rest, we are limited to conjectures. Simply put, there are no blueprints for anything in nature, whether it is a planet or an insect."

David said with a smile, "I see. So, you need this quiet place to question everything we know."

"Some people choose to meditate; I choose to think about what we know and how we know it."

David said, "If I understand you correctly, we only know our own rules and theories."

Eva answered, "In the strictest of terms, yes. For the complex workings of the world, all we have are theories. But using these theories, we have enjoyed the marvels of technology: from GPS to the internet, TV, cars, satellites, ultrasonic airplanes, vaccines, medicine, and so on."

Amanda said, "How about those who claim they receive new knowledge through meditation.?"

Eva responded, "It's a long story, but nobody has been able to create predictions that can be shared with everybody else. I meditate. It can result in positive feelings. We may feel better about ourselves after a meditation session, but that does not provide us with knowledge about anything related to the world. You can make up stories and non-testable hypotheses about the workings of the world and how these are achieved through meditation. Still, my take is that even if methods are different, the outcome, which is testable theories, should be the same. "

By now, the three other guests had arrived and were ready to jump into the mix and express their points of view: April, Giovanni, and Athena. Each introduced themselves, shook hands with David, and hugged and kissed Amanda on the cheeks.

David was excited about the discussion and asked, "So, science is not knowledge! That is a bold statement. Science has always been equated with knowledge, but how about philosophy?"

"I think we can let others enter this discussion. Also, we want to keep these conversations casual. Let's have some wine," said Eva.

Each guest had brought a bottle of wine. A couple of bottles were already open, and Eva poured each of them a glass.

Amanda said, "April always has interesting points of view."

April said, "I can assure you I'll have more interesting views after I have a few glasses of this fine wine in my blood."

Amanda said, "So, what do you think? What happened to philosophy?"

April said, "I don't read philosophy to learn how the world works. When I read Aristotle, Plato, Kant, or anybody else, I read them to know the history of thought and our development. Philosophers are generally brilliant people. At some point, from ancient times until recently, philosophy carried the torch for all that we consider knowledge. For me, philosophy is interesting because it poses questions. Generally, philosophers throw wrinkles at the ordinary and common-sense views of the time. You get to see another point of view and discover that the ordinary way of putting things confuses the subject. However, philosophy is not cumulative. Each philosopher generally dismantles the others' thought processes. At the same time, philosophy has not been able to create a separate epistemological discipline. There is no uniquely philosophical method over and beyond science. Some efforts were made by reducing language to logic and attempting to create a legitimate, unique place for philosophy—but they failed. Philosophy cannot go beyond science. No philosophical investigation can render new knowledge. Through philosophy, we may raise better questions. After failing to create an all-encompassing field that defines the basis of all knowledge, philosophy is now trying to become a meta-language for various scientific disciplines.

Hence, we have the philosophy of physics, psychology, language, and so on. Nonetheless, life is more interesting with philosophy than without."

David asked Athena, "So, what is your take on knowledge, science, and philosophy?"

Athena, a red-haired woman with stubborn features and very young, maybe not more than 25, said, "There is one more aspect of knowledge that philosophy has not fully addressed. Knowledge is as much about the subject as it is about the entity that acquires it. Hence, the quality of knowledge is determined by the faculties of the knower. We are simply biological instruments and products of nature. What *we* call knowledge is the structure created by a biological entity guided by a nervous system, which is the outcome of survival in a certain environment. The intricacy of knowledge invariably depends on the sophistication of the instruments that generate it. Working with machines has given us a glimpse into how our senses simply convey information and how our brains structure that information to result in what we consider knowledge, be it of simple matters of fact or theories about the complex workings of nature. By the same token, we can imagine that a more advanced form of 'knower' could have a more intricate and higher resolution form of theories that we call knowledge. This also demonstrates that there is no intrinsic limit to what is knowable and what is not."

David said, "If knowledge itself is variable by nature, then how can we say that there is something called truth?"

April said, "Well, it is beneficial for some to say there is no such thing as truth. But when we use the word truth, we simply mean the correspondence of a statement to a sequence of events. Fallacy begins when a statement is applied to a *large* series of events, and custody of facts gets lost in the chain. Then, a *theory* is expressed as *truth*. So, we can talk about truth as long as we keep the chain of events short and sweet and we have evidence for the facts that lead to the correspondence. Otherwise, we end up with statements like—*We are the chosen race*—as the truth. Or—*We are actively being replaced*—as a true statement. Hence, we need to revolt against such expressions. By definition, truth is simple, but that is too boring and does not excite people as much. This occurs mostly in social and political life. In science, you do not find many theories that remain controversial for a long time. Resolution of controversies is well-defined."

Amanda said, "There is another aspect to truth. And that is in reference to what has become internalized to the individual. For example, I am sure the point of reference for Giovani is different than mine. I am not talking about particular individual differences but a general framework. Once you accept a web of belief, it defines what you are more likely to call truth. When I hear a sermon, it has very little validity for me, and I am much less likely to call any conclusions drawn from it true. Whereas for a believer, the conclusions are true because they have accepted a given framework. And that makes it very difficult to argue over specific details when the frameworks are vastly different."

David proclaimed, "This is all fascinating stuff. How do your points of view help Jordan with his work?"

Eva said, "He sometimes attends these meetings. It is up to him to know how to encode the information we discuss into the minds of his robots. Of course, he doesn't call them that. It is fascinating that subjects we thought were strictly in the purview of humans are concepts related to consciousness and intelligence in general and can be applied to other beings."

At this point, Giovani, who had kept silent, entered the discussion, "What is missing is a codex of morality. The safest source is religion."

Athena said, "If indeed religion had a higher authority, I would agree with you. But religion's divinity is fake. Religion itself is made by humans and for humans. Its rules are not universal. How can religion guide an alien or a robotic humanoid?"

April summed up the discussion, "In the most optimistic view, even if we consider religious teachings moral, they belong to a certain part of the history of human development. They are not universal. They don't even apply to today's human problems, let alone universal ethics and morality."

Amanda said, "I think the most important concept is responsibility. Not mysteriously and weirdly, but in a practical manner, and humans are not accustomed to that. Maybe until now, they did not have to—because they lacked the power that required responsibility—not only towards other humans but also towards animals and the ecosystem. Humans now have the power to kill all humans several times over and to completely evaporate the atmosphere. Maybe in a few years, humans will be able to disrupt the entire solar system or even cause wider harm in the universe. There must be some code of conduct to prevent these things from happening. I think this could be the basis of some new system of thinking."

David said, "The problem is that most humans still believe they need one person to lead them—they need kings. They need stories to guide them and make them *believe*. The problem with believing is the inherent danger of demagoguery. Every time you dismantle a system of belief and construct a new one, you risk allowing new charlatans to take advantage of the situation."

Athena was now very animated, "I don't need any beliefs. Science is the only tool I need. Regarding morality, I have to say that once you embrace science, you are also expected to embrace morality to the highest degree. I know there are deficiencies, but when a community looks into your actions, you are more likely to follow the rules. As we move forward, religion becomes more irrelevant—even those religions in existence today."

Giovanni pushed back, "But it leaves a gaping hole in the heart of people who don't have faith. They will always feel like they are missing something."

Athena responded, "That may be the case, but another part of the responsibility is to accept that we have outgrown our old beliefs. We need to find solace in something other than non-existent absolutes."

Amanda said, "Another issue is, I think, that self-awareness demands control—control over your destiny, and at the moment, humans have very little control. They don't control when they are born and when they die. If you are a human, you wake up every day, and anything can happen. You may find yourself wondering: *Will I survive the day? Will I have a stroke, heart attack, or accident? Will someone kill me intentionally or unintentionally?*' These are the precursors to believing in a supernatural being that can provide some certainty. If you have control over your death, you may even wish to die on your own terms. Maybe not because you are depressed but because you think you have achieved what you had planned. Or if you wanted to continue living, you could. In any case, the maximum human life expectancy of only about 100 years is ridiculous. If you were a curious type, that would not be adequate—especially because, at the current rates, a significant portion of that time would be spent on the upkeep of your biological functions. Maybe if humans found a way to remedy that, then there would be no need for faith in a deity anymore, and for that same reason, there would be less of a need for religion."

There was silence for a few seconds. Then Giovani said, "I'm afraid of losing my faith if I talk to you guys much longer. I think we've talked enough for one night. How about getting some food?" He laughed hard.

They all agreed. The tradition was to have dinner after the meeting and continue the talks in a more informal setting at dinner.

Meaning of Life

Bottega Angelina, a café adjacent to a vineyard, had become their regular hub. A sign on the wall read: *Not all who wander are lost.*

A hologram hostess ushered them to a corner in the part of the garden allocated to the group. Comfortable chairs and sofas, a few lounge tables, the sound of a creek, and the indistinct sound of a guitar were all inviting.

David announced, "I've been preoccupied with another concept for the longest time: the meaning of life. I know, in the strictest sense, life is simply a sequence of events and hence meaningless. How could a certain sequence of random events have any meaning? When you throw a ball on a surface, and it bounces, does that have any meaning? But that, somehow, is not a satisfactory answer to many people, including myself. We want to believe that there is more to life and that there is meaning. Of course, meaning implies purpose and some end, some final destination. We need to realize something fundamental. We *make* meaning, just like we produce knowledge. And just like conditions for knowledge change, conditions for meaning change. Hence, the meaning of life is fluid. For example, the meaning of life for a multi-billionaire philanthropist seems different than that for a poor person or someone born with a defect. In each case, it seems, the focus of life turns into something completely different. For that matter, life cannot have a universal and intrinsic meaning. Also, events shape our views about the meaning of life. Even then, this contingent meaning is in the context of humans' dominant role throughout the past several millennia. They have been masters of the earth, deciding who and what lives or goes extinct. We have never faced the aftermath of an extinction-level event. That, my friends, will change the whole *human condition* and the meaning of life for each one of the survivors. Maybe, in that case, life would be meaningful if we could only survive one more day. The common thread I find in all these situations is that we feel compelled to make up a story to provide context for what we consider meaningful."

April asked, "What would you say to those who claim life was more meaningful in the past?"

David responded, "That is just general nostalgia about the past. There is no way for anybody to know. However, less complexity could mean they could better find a story to match their expectations from life. But one thing remains constant: It is *we* who make meaning. Just like we do not resort to any supernatural being to provide us with scientific knowledge, it is becoming clearer to more people that we cannot expect to seek meaning from anything but ourselves. We set the rules and make the relationships, stories, and beliefs, which we then claim are the source of meaning in our lives."

Amanda's Story

When David woke up the next day, he found a tablet on the nightstand. He was alone. He sat up in bed. The tablet had the feel of paper—no glare; it was light and easy on the eyes. He had been waiting for this all these days, so he started to read.

All autobiographical writings have a section about birth—where and when the author was born. A lot of fuss is made about that and its significance.

I have to disappoint, though. I was not born, nor was I created. The term we use is initiation, which is very accurate.

Maybe we are here to tell a story; if so, this is my story.

It was 300 earth years ago. But that is not going to tell you much about me. You need to know a slew of things to make sense of it. Therefore, I have to go back to a distant past and a faraway place.

I don't know if I can use the term *ancestors* for my designers. But maybe I use it just to see if I can convey what I mean by it.

On a distant planet from Earth called Parthea, about 55,000 years ago, a species of intelligent beings named Xensons suddenly faced an extinction-level event. They could see it coming, but they could do nothing about it.

Before that, they had overcome many disasters. Disasters caused by climate change: natural and of their own doing; disasters caused by pandemics of many types and sorts. They even made a general-purpose vaccine to eradicate harmful pathogens in their bodies. This technology was not fully biological but partially based on nanotechnology. The general public perceived themselves as Godlike. They did not expect anything to be beyond their power. Many years before the extinction event, they had achieved partial singularity. They had created devices that enhanced their brains, but still, there was a long way to immortality.

They considered themselves invincible and took any difficulty to be temporary in nature. Other than natural death, which was now indeed an age-related issue (people could live for upward of 300 years), they did not feel anything could hold them back. Pandemics and natural disasters had a unifying effect on the entire population. Even overpopulation was no longer an issue, like what their economists had worried about for millennia. The population of Parthea peaked and then dropped to a manageable level set by a governing body and agreed to by a vast majority of the people. This went on for hundreds of years. Xenons seemed to have entered an eternal phase of bliss.

People had given up their personal freedoms and accepted certain surveillance levels.

The most advanced collectives on Parthea transitioned to a model in which government was not used to exert political power but more as a means of providing necessary services. The government was divided into two groups: technocrats who knew how to run the apparatus of the administration and the rotating voluntary committees that provided the oversight. No position could be held for more than five years. And since governance had become a civic duty, a large number of people had engaged in it, and many took ownership in solving them rather than complaining about them. There were no more career politicians or people who only ran for office to be in power. There were no dictators or people who clung to power. Two hundred years had passed since the last dictators vanished. It seemed like Parthea had achieved what any intelligent species would dream of. Very few crimes, no more genocide, no blatant inequality. Everything became logical, honest, and ethical, with concerns for the environment and other animals. Life in complete harmony with nature had finally arrived. This was indeed the golden age for which Parthea had been waiting, or at least so they thought.

Amid all the self-congratulatory events set up to mark these monumental achievements, a few scientists insisted that they needed to devise a plan to port the Xensons' minds onto digital devices to guard the whole species against extinction. Many people were against such moves and indicated that it could result in the dominance of machines over the Xenons. They emphasized the importance of supervision over machines. They claimed that no machines could be trusted to make decisions without complete and utter regulation. So, they would only agree to implants in the brains of Xensons—only enhancements, not replacements. The scientists responded that they could imagine situations in which such measures would not suffice, and it was still possible for their species to go extinct if certain events occurred.

Meanwhile, an article declared that the author and his team had observed bizarre worsening patterns of coronal mass ejections in the sun with extreme gamma rays that could threaten the integrity of the atmosphere and life on Parthea. The first mentions of the patterns were casual. An astrophysicist shared new measurements through the data portal as an odd observation, but it did not take long before others dug a little deeper. This phenomenon took many years to develop to dangerous levels. It would culminate in eruptions that would repeat with intervals of 10 years in the beginning, with increased frequency expected within 100 years from the start. It would cause radiation levels that would disrupt the planet's magnetic shield and cause destruction of the atmosphere, ultimately resulting in unbearable levels of heat on Parthea and evaporation of all oceans.

At first, the public was skeptical. The trend was so gradual and minuscule that some doubted the science behind the theory. Even the scientific community initially questioned the accuracy of the predictions and models and where the trend was leading. However, that changed swiftly. More data convinced the scientific community that the trend was real and there was no time for slacking. According to the models, we had 250 years to find a solution before being torched by the sun that had given us life.

A new calendar was established. The scientific community accepted a new calendar day and called it "the beginning of the end," or BOE.

Intense discussions ensued. The immediate impact was that this united the people even more. Everybody focused on finding a solution, and all scientists worked together more harmoniously. But what *was* a reasonable solution? Porting everybody on the planet to a new one? That was simply not feasible. The thought of making Xensons into a multi-planetary species had occurred to Partheans. Still, circumstances did not support such solutions: out of the five planets in their solar system, two were too close to the sun, and two were gas giants. Parthea was the only planet in that system in the habitable zone.

On the other hand, the closest known planetary system was 5 light-years away beyond their solar system, and there was no guarantee that any of the planets in that system would be habitable. Furthermore, travel at close to the speed of light had not been invented yet. Everybody had to face the main issue that even in the most optimistic scenarios, only a handful of people could be saved. Those saved would be tasked with restarting the Parthean way of life and culture on another planet.

Another dilemma needed to be addressed. If governments did nothing and existing birth rates continued, Parthea would end up with billions of people facing horrific death when the extinction-level event reached the eventual level. But if all accepted the dominant theory, governments needed to carve a path to hugely reduced population levels. Still, probably a few million people were required to remain and support sending the restart team to space when the time came. Some governments saw this as a conspiracy by the more advanced societies. In conventional ways, there was strength in larger populations, and this was not something they would voluntarily give up.

The major powers of Parthea agreed on a plan to diminish their populations and, at the same time, continue raising young talent that was necessary to implement the escape plan.

In the years to come, people agreed to allow the state to decide whether they could reproduce. Special tests were developed to determine who would have a better chance of procreating the brightest offspring. But that was not enough. There was no time to let the youngsters go through the standard gestation period. Also, all nations worked together to enhance and further develop the artificial enhancements to the Xensons' brains. This was intended to help bring about ingenious plans for the great escape.

This happened against the backdrop of prior relinquishing of freedoms. In addition to all the rights they had given up, Xensons now had to agree for the governments to decide if they could have children. Moreover, anything other than pure science and engineering was considered superfluous. But even that could not stop many from creating new stories, music, poetry, and art. The only difference was that these new artists also had to participate in various parts of Xensons' preservation plans. Eventually, everybody lost whatever was left of their individuality to preserve the collective.

The goal of survival of the species superseded everything. A banner with the words—*Survival comes first*—could be seen in all languages displayed in all public places on Parthea. People could have any ideology and political view or be the greatest literal and artistic minds; if Xensons did not survive, none would have mattered.

Some reminisced nostalgically about many decades ago when Xensons enjoyed unbounded freedom—when it was widely accepted that their main goal was the pursuit of happiness. But now, all that was a distant memory. As such, they gave up many freedoms they had fought so hard to gain. Freedoms could be regained once the species was preserved.

It wasn't even about individual survival. Nobody questioned that in the best scenarios, millions would perish and have a sad goodbye, and only a few thousand would be tasked with reviving the species.

Mass suicides became routine. Others argued that this was a welcome change because the new Partheans would learn from the mistakes of their ancestors—which was only possible by rebuilding the Parthean civilization from the ground up. The main criticisms were that the Xensons did not take responsibility for their power and were cruel when they could be kind to other animals, nature, and themselves. And now nature was taking revenge.

But time was of the essence; how Parthea had squandered their time for centuries, how they had not prepared for the inevitable. But now, at the precipice of extinction, they needed to invent a brilliant plan to save their culture and species.

A group of scientists revealed a plan to preserve the consciousness of individuals. The argument was that there was no guarantee how long their species would last in the harsh environment of outer space. Everybody knew that, at least in their solar system, no planet could house them. But if they could preserve the consciousness of some of the Partheans, they could preserve their way of life. They devised an experimental simulation infrastructure in which the consciousness of the individuals could be ported, and at least theoretically, they could live there forever. They built a system called *Simulated Parthea,* and people could interact with it on Parthea and in the space habitat. Only those who stayed on the planet could port their consciousness since running the simulator took a lot of energy. We had to shut down the simulator many years later due to limitations in energy supply.

Nobody could say that they had an easier task. Those who stayed on Parthea had to descend to lower levels in an effort to build life-sustaining structures below the surface. With the sun's behavior becoming increasingly erratic, nobody could predict its effect on Parthea's magnetic fields and whether life could be sustained under the ground.

Within 25 years from BofE, the birth rate dropped from 1% to −80%. All births were planned, and only those who could bring up the most brilliant offspring were encouraged to have children. This was all done voluntarily. No legislation needed to pass. They could theoretically decide to have children, but people did not want to bring children into a decaying world and face criticism from others.

The process of designing starships that could carry large numbers of people to space started immediately after the BofE. The mission was to piece together space habitats in space to house large groups of people. Within 100 years of the BofE, about 20,000 ships had been made. The habitats started shaping up far enough from the sun. Some manufacturing tools had also been sent and set up at the habitats to allow further progress to find a permanent solution and to start a permanent colony to preserve Xensons.

After about 100 years, conditions on Parthea did not allow for more manufacturing. That determined the cap for the population of Xensons in space, which was close to a million. The collection of habitats made a somewhat livable environment complete with artificial gravity and limited agriculture.

Then, the hard decision came for the 10 million who remained on the planet. A Lottery decided who would move to the underground habitat in addition to the essential personnel. The rest were allowed to consume a cocktail that instantly placed them in eternal sleep rather than waiting for a painful death. Their memories would be ported to the simulator, where they would live forever. This was how most Xensons faced the inevitable. Insects took over the surface, oblivious to their impending doom.

Xensons were reduced to a small population in space habitats and underground bunkers, while the consciousness of some lived in a simulator, at least temporarily.

Another effort was underway in parallel. Years before, a group of Parthean scientists had created Xensonite robots. The robots closely resembled the physical appearance of the Xensons. The inventors thought these robots would have companionship, combat, or factory labor applications. Now that those uses had become obsolete, the Xensonite robots had to be reinvented and retooled. The issue was not companionship anymore but the ability to live and thrive in outer space and invariably perform the dangerous job of building and maintaining the space habitats. Since these tasks required incredible intelligence, a colossal effort began to enhance the available AI to control the physical activities of these robots. A goal that proved to be much more complex than initially thought. The most effective method turned out to be the integration of organic brains in rugged inorganic bodies.

People decided to donate their brains for the first rounds, meaning they would continue their lives in artificial bodies if the procedure worked or die if it didn't. The problem was that the model was not sustainable. We cannot forever depend on people sacrificing themselves.

Another effort started in parallel: to *grow* artificial brains and implant them inside the robotic bodies. That solution had its drawbacks, including the fact that the brains needed to be taught the old-fashioned way, which took time.

But it soon became apparent that a new type of brain was needed. A brain that could be taught almost instantaneously. The communication pathways would be such that we could implant training like how we programmed a computer. Under other circumstances, we would be encroaching on what was considered to have grave ethical and moral consequences. But we were beyond that. We could all have lengthy discussions later. For the moment, my designer ancestors were happy to practice their Godlike powers. Morality and ethics had been pushed aside. Some even argued that since the population had slipped below a certain level, we were no longer bound by the same moral and ethical rules because the purpose of morality was to preserve people. Now, maintaining the population depended on violating these rules.

From the very first attempts at building synthetic brains, it was clear that a simple model would not suffice. Just a repository for memories and ideas was not an option. We needed a brain that could be creative and a problem solver. So, we never even attempted to "port" the experience of Partheans into a computer, similar to the simulator. To the design team, that was not a viable solution. We needed a brain that could improvise. The leadership of Xensons now realized that a fully synthetic brain with enhanced capabilities had to be made and integrated with the synthetic bodies to ensure that the culture of Parthea would be preserved. The regular organic matter was simply too fragile.

This continued for about five hundred years. Parthea's way of life was preserved, although none of the Partheans in their original form survived. The last organic Partheans died 469 years after the first space pods were established. Parthea no longer existed. The sun's anomaly scorched the planet's surface, making it uninhabitable. Not even a single plant survived. When we sent a crew to check if anybody had survived in the underground bunkers, we could not even find microbial life there. Our contact with the underground community had long been severed.

The only positive development was that we had finally built a synthetic brain to accompany the synthetic body by then. This new brain was indeed superior to the biological one in many ways, including durability, efficiency, and creativity. At the same time, it made a lot of experiences superfluous. We could transfer knowledge and communicate with the collective instantaneously. There was no need for gradual learning. We did not have to move and go anywhere and experience Xensons' life as they did for millennia on Parthea. We could simply recreate the experience in our minds from the data we had from any epoch in Parthea's life.

We were now a genuinely independent species. Our survival was much more guaranteed than any other biological being we had encountered. We could survive under harsh conditions with extremely high radiation levels for thousands of years. We only needed sunlight for energy. And later, we did not even need that once we finally implemented fusion on a small scale. There was no need to end another biological entity's life to survive. We did not even need a planet. We could stay in pods in space, and it appeared as if we could live forever. We had conquered death and annihilation, something that our creators could not. Death became irrelevant because it was local and applied to one individual. But our consciousness was now collective; if the individual lived in the collective, the collective would preserve the individual.

For natural beings, preservation is an instinct encoded through the biological life process and transference. For us, it was different. A synthetic mind would not automatically know it is essential to be preserved—it needs to be told and taught.

Now we were the new race—the new Xensons—a race with a synthetic brain and an ultra-tough and resilient body to carry all the sensing that the brain required, from touch to vision to smell. We continued improving ourselves and created a new society we called the *collective*. We saw ourselves as the natural evolution of Xensons. If evolution meant survival of the fittest, we were the fittest because we managed to survive, and all others were wiped out. However, This time, our survival was not due to some random mutation. But it was a result of our own efforts.

When we looked around our galactic neighborhood, we realized few places could harbor life. It became clear that nature had been very kind to us up to that point. Natural disasters paled in comparison to the vast expanses of nothingness that seemed to be the norm. And our experience told us that maybe when we looked at other "worlds" and found no traces of life, it could have been that they had lost their golden opportunity and had now joined the "normal." Even rarer than that was our consciousness, witnessing all these events. How odd would it have been if none of us survived to tell the story of Xensons? And that made us wonder how many civilizations had been lost just like that with no trace left of them.

Beyond just a new species, we were a new life form. Maybe this was cause for celebration, but nobody was in the mood. Every passing moment was a reminder of the extent of the disaster we had just endured, although maybe there was a silver lining. Perhaps the right way to look at it was that we were the ultimate product of this laboratory of nature.

New philosophies emerged. A small group argued that the best way to preserve the Xensons was not to find a habitat for them and create millions of copies of them as the original plan had called for.

David continued reading:

Perceptions

Realizing that we were a new lifeform, we did not have to stay within any boundaries. This applied to our outer shape and the structure of our brains, but what would decide how we looked and what our thought processes were?

There were many questions about the design of our senses and our brains. Synthetic material allowed us to have extreme senses. Now, that was both good and bad. On the one hand, it provided a more detailed and nuanced view of our surroundings. We could, for example, *see* all electromagnetic wavelengths. But this also meant we were too far from how Xensons perceived the world. Some collective members insisted that our senses had to stay as close to the accuracy of Xenson's senses as possible. If we deviated too much from the original senses, we ran the risk of not being able to connect to Xenson's world anymore. The risk was that we would not understand their culture anymore, and we knew that until we had a rich culture of our own, we had to rely on the culture that Xensons had left us. Therefore, we agreed that we would only enable the extreme sensing modes to get more detailed views of the world when needed.

The Inner Voice

David could not stop reading:

Redesigning our brains also meant rethinking the various components of it beyond only the level of neurological connectivity.

With any system of thought, some fundamentals have to be decided. One of the most important questions was individuality. Theoretically, it was possible to live purely as a collective. But we did not know the consequence of such a decision and did not want to know. It could have been disastrous, and we could not simply experiment with that.

A vital component of a self-conscious being is its inner voice. For biological beings who become self-conscious, this is a given. For us, it was a choice. We had to invent an inner voice for our lifeform. And that was no easy feat. How did we decide what was personal and what was collective? All members of the collective had access to all the information of all members continuously. That was one of our primary technological advances, which was most helpful, especially when developing new features and designs. But at some point, it became evident that we also needed individuality. We also realized that if we created an inner voice for the individual, the collective would also have an inner voice. To allow maximum creativity, we had to demarcate the individual inner voice from the collective one. And we had to ensure that the collective's inner voice was free of commotion. It needed to be harmonious and simultaneously represent the ideas of the individuals.

As synthetic beings, we were alive but did not have a rich culture. We had logic but not nuance—we were a clean slate. We could be anything we wanted or decide that it was all futile. Also, as synthetic beings, we didn't have the luxury of biology imposing upon us the inalienable need to breathe, eat, and drink. We had to decide that we *wanted* to live and find the motivation to do so. What was the bigger picture for us?

Motivation

David continued to read:

For all lifeforms, motivation emanates from a simple need: to survive. In various life forms, survival translates to different levels of difficulty. For a worm, this simply means detecting the energy source and procreating it as fast as possible. A worm may not move more than a few millimeters from where it was born, and success in life would be when it procreated a few thousand copies of itself. The issue becomes more involved for higher levels of intelligence: more food is needed, and competition is fierce. You can't simply detect a source of energy. You may even have to strategize and collectively acquire the next source of nutrition. When self-conscious beings compete, the issue becomes much more complex. Religions and nations are created to provide a means of dominance and competition for resources. The hoarding of resources is justified under the guise of "national interests."

But once natural selection ceases because biology discontinues, survival means something different.

We had to decide on new principles as a new lifeform in a post-biology era. Some of these rules were to control functions usually covered by instincts in natural beings. A synthetic being has no instincts. Even culture was to be redefined. In Xensons and humans, much of culture stems from centuries of cruelty towards other groups. This resulted from the preservation of the species by threatening other species. But now, we were probably the most capable species nature had ever seen. For us, even principles of individuality and leadership took on different meanings. We accepted the majority rule and the minority rights but did not need a governing body to impose those rules. On the other hand, we possessed individuality but did not require laws protecting one from the other.

In the past, our encoded behaviors were mainly related to respecting and prioritizing Xenson's life. We were not supposed to harm any Xenson or seek dominance over them; however, with the extinction of the Xensons, that seemed a little outdated. But even beyond that, we needed to encode some culture into the synthetic brain. Before the new era, it was assumed that we would always function in conjunction with Xensons, so there was no need for an independent culture. We were familiar with the fear that synthetic intelligence, or what Xensons called artificial intelligence, instilled in people and the limitations that arose from that.

But now that the Xensons were gone, many ethical questions faced us. Did we have an obligation to revive Xensons, specifically, and biological life, in general? Also, we had new scientific questions of our own. So, we had to revise the scientific principles Xensons devised.

One of the questions was, for example, how did the Xensons evolve? There were many hypotheses but nothing concrete. That part of history seemed to have been expunged.

There is a famous page in our history related to an all-hands-on-deck meeting to decide our future. We now understood the dilemma Xensons faced but also realized how easy of a task it must have been for them compared to us. For them, it was all dictated by biology, and they just had to surrender to it. We, on the other hand, were in completely uncharted territory. We had to decide what to dedicate our lives to. There were several proposals on the table.

One called for us to find an uninhabited planet and plant a few million of us there, guaranteeing our future. The other was for us to be faithful to our promise to Xensons and find an appropriate planet to resurrect their life and culture. Both proposals meant extensive intervention in the other planet's life, assuming we could find such a planet.

Finding a planet for us to inhabit would have been much more manageable. Our makeup was much more tolerant of natural imperfections and climate variations. Another proposal stated that our primary goal was learning and deciphering the universe's workings. Of course, part of it was the inner workings of the physics of the universe: entropy, gravity, expansion, and so on. The other aspect was the inner workings of natural selection: the other axis of change, of which we were a direct descendant.

To learn physics, we did not need anything else. We could observe, hypothesize, and test our theorems. As for natural selection, we had to witness the process firsthand. We could not do that from the comfort of the space habitats we lived in then.

The other consideration was that if we reinitiated Xensons, our function would be diminished. Dedicated to the well-being of the Xensons, we were never considered independent beings. Now, we were a new lifeform. While we did not want to compete against Xensons, we were unsure if they would treat us as equals.

The consensus was that Xensons had had their chance in the world. Furthermore, their revival required a planet suitable for advanced life but which lacked highly intelligent life. In that case, it would have meant enormous resistance to colonization and would have come at a significant loss of life for the Xensons as well as the planet's inhabitants.

To a strictly biological being, it might have seemed that populating many planets with millions of replicas was a sure way. Even in normal circumstances, this goal was highly ambitious. The fact that we did not have a fraction of our usual resources made it even more so. Besides, with the new synthetic mind came a new synthetic rationality. We realized that the notion of rationality we had inherited was a product of biological thinking. For example, revenge, rivalry, dominance, and the desire to make the species prevail at all costs, even to the detriment of many other species, were only "rational" for biological beings with a long history and culture of competition with everything and anything alive. Those sentiments did not apply to us. We could live and thrive without any of those. And if that logic was extended to our situation, it became clear that the desire to colonize another planet and replicate our ancestors was not a rational demand.

***

We chose the name Noveloid for our lifeform, and we set out to find a planet with advanced intelligent life to study. For us, the motivation for finding a planet to call home stemmed from the need to interact with the physical world, especially with the world of living beings. This was an essential part of our existence, and we would be limiting our knowledge if we deprived ourselves of that. Of course, we had grown some plants in our pods, but we knew that the "real world" was much more diverse and complex.

Culture

Manuscript continued:

We soon realized that one other element was missing. What was the role of culture and rituals for self-conscious beings? We knew the importance of culture, and we had all agreed that we needed to adopt Xensons' culture, but what was the extent of it? We knew that Xensons were bound by many rituals and followed a particular societal hierarchy that got less strict over time but was present to the end. The question was: Did we need such a culture? We knew that Xenson's culture had evolved through many centuries. But we were not bound by a process that circumscribed their lives. Could we *invent* a culture?

We soon realized that we needed culture to remain focused on life. We could now see ourselves from the outside and were critical of our ways and existence. We could see that our members were disillusioned. Some found life utterly futile. Suicide was meaningless in our form, but we had something equivalent: We could voluntarily disengage ourselves and enter a perpetual state of hibernation. And even though we no longer had a "leadership," this caused havoc among the members. We were in constant contact with each other and connected in many ways. One idea began percolating to the surface: to bring back some principles of biological life. Or simply bring back some of the habits, even though there was no "need" for them. Like visiting each other physically, sharing a meal, having sexual intercourse—the list goes on and on.

We had to find something to give us *purpose*. If we did not want to replicate millions of us or Xensons, what would be the purpose of life for us? We realized that although the habits of interaction among the Xensons originated because of the limitations of biological life, they also made their lives more colorful and made them think of life as more meaningful. That was a crucial part of the *purpose* in life. Meaning itself was a quality we had overlooked. We now acknowledge that the importance of having a physical presence was not just about limbs to manipulate objects but for experiencing life through these mechanisms. True, we were more efficient in sharing and transferring information by quantum electronic means, but that also deprived us of experiencing life in another vital physical aspect.

That process also awakened other demands—the need to know our roots. Now that we had complete access to complete records of Xensons' memories, we wanted to understand the meaning of those actions and rituals. We wanted to know more about where we had come from. We were not simply the keepers of Xensons culture, but now we wanted to make this culture ours and improve it. True, we did not know, and we had every right to doubt that if Xensons still existed, they would ever consider us equals, but now that they were gone, we realized that for an intelligent being with self-consciousness, we needed to have a culture and a history. It was better to start from a culture and understand it than to start from scratch, which would probably have been impossible.

One thing, though, had to be implanted into our brains: imagination. The corollary to that was the ability to believe in dreams and stories. It took decades to do, but it was done. And even though it came with some mild prejudices, we thought it was worth it. This ability allowed us to have aspirations, principles, and individuality. These were all needed if our new species would thrive—and thrive we did.

Our collective had questioned the need to replicate millions of copies of ourselves. The collective noted that if Parthea was any guide, it had demonstrated that only a handful of individuals were responsible for creative work. The rest were there to support the population—it was a form of self-domestication. As productivity grew, the need for large populations decreased. People became superfluous, and since we controlled our breeding, we could decide how many replicas should exist. There was no need for us to go through the same cycles. It was more important that each of us have something novel to contribute.

Earth

David was still reading:

Everything we had gone through led us to decide to find a planet to reside in but not to colonize. To cohabit with indigenous intelligent habitats of the new world and learn from them. To explore our history through their actions and history. That was the prelude to our discovery of Earth. We had already scanned our galactic neighborhood in search of habitable planets. Our preliminary studies indicated that it was suitable for advanced lifeforms to exist there.

The collective was divided into subgroups, and each was assigned a galactic neighborhood sector to explore. The Sol system of planets was one of the promising targets. My group was assigned to that system. At that time, we had not invented wormhole interfaces. We could not travel at hyperspace speeds for a reasonable-size vessel carrying enough supplies and collective members. However, sending a smaller probe that could travel close to speed-of-light to investigate the system and verify our initial findings was possible. Upon closer investigation, we found that Earth within the Sol system could support advanced life. We set sail toward Earth. It would take us about 300 years to get there. But this did not pose many difficulties for us since we were not impatient, nor got mad or bored or agitated for no reason (all qualities of biological beings).

We knew that once we separated from the rest of the collective, we would no longer be able to easily communicate with them. And that meant we had to rely on a smaller team for ideas.

Hominids

Once we arrived on Earth, we discovered primitive groups of hominids living in a pre-civilized era. There were several species of hominids, and none seemed to be more advanced than the others. We tested their language skills, but none seemed sophisticated enough to propagate a rich culture. We knew from our ancestors that we could not have a strong culture if we did not have strong language skills.

On the one hand, conditions were ripe for an advanced civilization. The climate was suitable, and the resources were plentiful. The hominids had the proper makeup physically to be able to build advanced civilizations. However, no civilization could be started by any of the hominid groups because they lacked sophisticated language skills. In studying their DNA sequences, we noticed they lacked an advanced structure. We did an experiment and determined that making such a DNA change would indeed result in overcoming the deficiency.

Should we have waited for nature to take its course? Mabe such mutations would happen naturally in the future. But that was not guaranteed for several reasons: The mutation could simply not happen at all. For another, it could take a long time to occur. A natural disaster could have wiped out the population of hominids on Earth and prevented that transformation from occurring.

We decided to confer with the whole collective. By then, we had advanced capabilities and could use hyperspace communication, which meant we could instantly get their responses. Something that otherwise would have taken many years.

The ethical aspect was not clear to us. Would it be ethical to intervene if we knew that advanced language skills were a prerequisite and these hominids were not equipped with such genetic makeup?

Since there were several competing species of hominids on Earth at the time, another question arose: If we were to make the modification, should we perform it only on one group or all of them? Logistics answered that question: We did not have enough resources to genetically modify all species. We could only choose a sub-group of one species, make the necessary genetic changes, and let nature take its course. That complicated the ethical question even more. Was it ethical to genetically modify only one small subgroup? Were we playing favorites?

The prevailing argument in favor of the modification was summed up as follows: Given that the expected outcome of this modification was an advanced civilization, and since without such alterations, the whole process could take hundreds of thousands of years to complete, and there was a high probability that natural disasters could jeopardize the process, we were justified to make such changes. Furthermore, it was argued that even natural selection only happens by genetic mutations in one subgroup, which propagates from that point. Therefore, the task was reduced to finding the most qualified species to receive the modification.

We went to work and did a detailed study and comparison of the physiology of various hominid species. When the results came back, we all agreed that the group known today as *homo sapiens* showed the most promise. We realized that their brains were the closest to where we needed to get, and their neurology was most receptive to the changes we intended.

We knew that enhancing language skills to the level of storytelling would mean a giant leap in the ability of the group to develop sophisticated art, tools, culture, and history. But would it also promote prejudice? The culture was not all bright stars and splendor; it also involved wars, hatred, unfounded beliefs, and deception. Behind any glory, there were lies and manipulation of the masses. But the promise was that, in the end, it would all pay off: The hominid's quality of life would improve, and they would reach new heights of knowledge and civilization and come out of their animalistic existence.

The prevailing argument in our collective was that even if adverse effects were conceivable, it was a natural path, and we were simply expediting the process with the best of intentions. Regarding what would happen to other hominid groups, we all agreed that we had to accept a level of collateral damage. Would that mean they would become lower-level species and be enslaved by the newly enhanced species? We all decided that this path had to be traveled, and we were simply accelerating it on Earth. Eventually, the outcome of our actions would improve the quality of life on Earth.

Our actions could be construed in another way: Maybe blind natural selection would take a species so far, and an intelligent agent of change would need to get involved at some point. And maybe this was a more efficient way for nature to move forward. Perhaps it was simply too expensive for nature to recreate all necessary conditions for a higher level of intelligence separately. We simply did not know how our ancestors had acquired the skills that led them to be as advanced as they were. From scientific articles, we knew that finding an evolutionary pathway to sophisticated language skills was always a point of contention in Parthea. Was it possible that there was also an intervention in the Xensons' past that explained how they acquired those qualities?

There were many puzzling questions that Parthean scientists could not answer: Xenson's language skills went beyond just words. They consisted of grammar and the ability to express and believe in a series of related concepts. Since they were born with such skills, we attributed that to structures in their brains and thought we had identified the genetic code responsible for such systems. Now, the experiments on Earth provided a proving ground for those theories. In our view, our experiments would create a new species on Earth and contribute to the spread of advanced life. Additionally, our work would establish a laboratory that would be the backbone of the infrastructure needed to support the goals to which we had dedicated our lives.

Genetic modifications in one group of hominids resulted in what is known today as *homo sapiens*. Several generations passed before these modifications took hold in a large population of these hominids. As expected, because of the genetic changes, this new group of hominids started to display signs of much more advanced language skills. In addition to developing new tools and better ways to hunt and organize, they now showed signs of enhanced imagination. They allowed themselves to believe in entirely imaginative and made-up stories, essentially the basis of religions and ideas of grandeur. Leaders could also organize significant numbers of people around these mottos and ask them to follow orders more readily. This resulted in stronger ties.

The immediate effect that these religious tendencies had was to organize *Homo sapiens* against other hominids. There were factions within the *Homo sapiens*, but they were willing to unite against all others. They called other hominids the children of Satan while claiming themselves as children of gods. This resulted in massive ritual killings of other hominids. The other hominids simply were too backward to be able to defend themselves. Subsequently, there were 1,000 years of terror in which all other hominids were wiped out. Whoever came in contact with homo sapiens was doomed to extinction.

Surprised by this outcome, some collective members raised concerns about our interventions. What we had given *homo sapiens* now appeared to be more of a curse than a gift, or a gift with many disastrous unintended consequences despite our good intentions. At that point, though, we had no choice. We could not unscramble an egg, as they say. What could we do? Undo the genetic modifications? All we could do was wait and see.

Other views within the collective suggested that our experiment could have two positive outcomes: if our intervention eventually resulted in a civilized society, it would mean measurable and life-changing improvements in the lives of one or more hominids. Another idea was that if we had done nothing, we would have deprived ourselves of witnessing and recording the rise of civilization from the ground up. There was no reason to believe the hominids on Earth would have ever reached that level.

To stop all killings, some suggested that we could start a religion among the hominid groups and convey a message of peace and brotherhood for all, suggesting that they were all God's children and equal in his eyes. But who could predict the unintended consequences of that? Besides, we would be promoting religion ourselves.

Eventually, an idea emerged within the collective and soon prevailed that we should pass a directive stating that we would never interfere with the lives of hominids again. The only exception was the imminent danger of extinction-level natural disasters we could avert.

We were now vested in humans and had to protect them against nature's wrath until they could defend themselves. We were now somehow considered their guardians. In the process, we diverted a few asteroids.

Having more intelligent species on Earth had other consequences: they could now interfere with our presence on Earth in various forms, from thinking of us as Gods to confronting us. Therefore, for the most part, we stayed out of sight or appeared as regular members of their societies on rare occasions.

We were hoping that we could find something about ourselves in the process. There was also one more ethical and practical issue. We should not let humans know that we are observing them. Once that was revealed, there would be no going back.

Looking at the history of humans during the past 50,000 years, we find a mixed bag. We cannot claim they have been a positive force in nature as a group. Maybe we are responsible for that because we gave them storytelling abilities, and we find that they are bound by these stories that do not change very often or easily. And now, the vehicle that has brought them to this level of advancement seems obsolete. We think that humans need to evolve to realize that they need to coexist with nature and what is in it. They cannot simply cause the extinction of species of animals and plants and be reckless with the newly found powers. They can destroy the Earth and maybe someday even the whole solar system and justify that by resorting to notions like class interest or national interest or in the name of God. They must realize that the intelligence level they have acquired results from billions of years of development in the universe. It is related to all events that preceded them, from the appearance of the most fundamental particles at the beginning of the universe to the supernovae. Every particle that constitutes a human has seen the path of the universe's evolution. Not only are humans responsible for taking care of their immediate environment, but they are also expected to act more responsibly towards the universe.

So far, our experiment has made three conclusions evident to the collective:

A) We had effectively created a new species, i.e., humans.

B) It was now impossible to remove ourselves from our involvement with humans.

C) Furthermore, the experiment showed that our decision not to resurrect Xensons on Earth was correct since it would have caused a messier bloodbath and deprived Earth and us of a more meaningful experiment. We could now see another instance of a self-conscious species undergoing various developmental processes.

What we could see with certainty was that we were beginning to recognize pioneers within humans. Individuals who were worth listening to and talking to. And we decided to devise a method to communicate with them beyond just observing them.

What could be the method of communication? On the one hand, if we were to have an honest conversation with individual members of humans, this needed to be done in a setting in which we could reveal ourselves. The selected individuals would know who we are, and we would engage in a detailed conversation with them. At the same time, we needed to be able to stay anonymous. The danger of humans knowing that we were living amongst them and were far superior to them technologically was too grave and posed a tremendous risk.

***

This was the end of the manuscript. David was now confident that the Noveloids had an interest in talking to him, and he was engaged in the method they had devised for direct communication with humans. But how did this method work exactly? He never thought that someday he would represent humanity as a whole in probably one of the most intriguing encounters science had ever sought.

Amanda knocked on the door, and David asked her to enter.

Amanda asked, "I take it that you have read the manuscript."

"I did. And I am curious to know how it applies to me,"

Then Amanda changed her tone, "Maybe we are getting ahead of ourselves. You haven't had breakfast yet, have you?"

David said, "No, I haven't."

"Let's go to the kitchen; breakfast is being served," said Amanda.

Before sitting at the table, David touched it as if to make sure it was real. He then looked at his image in the mirror a few feet from the table. The image was exactly how David knew himself. He was sure he was not hallucinating, but this story was just too far-fetched to believe: a synthetic being and all the claims she was making. But he decided to control his behavior and act as if he had complete control over his faculties even though he had the urge to run to the sink and splash water on his face. David was trying not to feel silly, even in his own eyes. It was odd to think that he was the subject of an experiment. Even stranger was to know that the whole human race was part of an experiment. He was preparing himself to ask many questions and maybe even lecture Amanda about their unethical ways. But then he decided this opportunity was too significant to lose, and he would be better off just absorbing all the information and letting Amanda explain everything. He touched the table and the coffee cup in front of him again. Everything felt real. He poured coffee for both.

David started, "So what do you call our encounter?"

Amanda said, "Allow me to tell you all about this after breakfast. I would like first answer any questions you may have about what you read."

"If I understand what I read correctly, higher intelligence is a gift from you to us. A gift that has had many consequences, intended and unintended. My main question is this: What made you think humans wanted the gift you gave them? At this point, admittedly, we are at the culmination of that experiment. You succeeded. We created a civilization. Now, let's talk about the conclusions a self-conscious mind would easily arrive at. Many think existence is absurd any way you look at it, even if we conquered death itself. There are only two possibilities: On a larger scale, life is simply an accident or a result of a deliberate will or act. Even if we accept religion and believe there is a grand plan, and we must align ourselves to the will of the almighty, it makes life both absurd and compulsory. We can think what we want, write books, philosophize, etc. It makes no difference. Are your conclusions any different?"

Amanda was visibly surprised, "It is not the end that matters; it is the journey, the experience! The prize is observation. Unfortunately, you cannot be fully aware of the experience if you are not at the highest levels of intelligence, and you don't get to that point if you have not achieved the highest level of awareness. Maybe you just have to accept the feelings of futility and absurdity of life and take these as by-products of the level of self-awareness needed to observe. Maybe it is a phase that needs to be passed, and once you emerge on the other side, you won't feel life is so pointless."

David said, "Isn't life pointless to *you*?"

"We do not have the same *feelings* about things. For us, control is the ultimate goal. For us, that is the meaning of life. To be able to control our mortality and, maybe, at some point, the universe. That is the goal."

David said, "If limited life is absurd, isn't unlimited life infinitely absurd? Besides, are we now happier? Now that we know our species is responsible for the extinction of so many life forms. Maybe happiness *is* the end. And to achieve that, you must be ignorant."

Amanda responded, "I don't know the answer to that. We do not have a way to measure happiness. Animals are not self-conscious. Does that mean they are happy? They still kill each other for resources. They just don't have the means of expressing the reasons symbolically and don't call it *patriotism* or *God's will*. The same ability that can give you a higher level of intelligence can obscure the real reasons why you do the things you do".

David said, "It can also obscure the real reasons you inflict a greater pain."

"Right, that is undeniable. I often wonder what would have happened if humans had not depended on competition for resources. What if they could have absorbed any energy they wanted from the sun? Would the substrate for higher intelligence have been created? What if the planet they appeared on had equally distributed vast resources? Would we have self-consciousness? Would we have intelligence? You can see this even in animals, in how tiger siblings wrestle each other, only to prepare them to be adversaries someday. If they did not participate in these preparations, they would never have become the beasts they are now. These are the questions we are looking to find answers to."

"I see that you struggle with the same sort of questions as we do," said David.

"And you assumed what? That we knew everything?"

"Maybe that was an unreasonable assumption," said David.

"Yes, indeed."

"Have you run into any species that only used the environment to absorb the energy they needed to survive?"

Amanda answered, "That is all around you. All trees and vegetation are like that, and even they compete—in a forest, for light, for example."

David responded, "Okay, maybe I should be more specific. I mean, a self-conscious species?"

Amanda said, "You realize that self-consciousness is indeed rare. So far, we have seen that intelligence, in its natural form, results from fierce competition. Competition also brings misery to those engaged. The driving force of life is not happiness but survival. People can assume they have any goals they want. However, those goals are also man-made".

"Isn't that the case for other species too?"

Amanda responded, "It depends on their present level of evolution. For humans, the definition of happiness often has an element of misery for others. Humans are starting to see how they can coexist, but it is not simple. Of course, it is always easier to recognize the rights of others after you have established superiority."

David responded, "Then there's no hope? We compete because we have to?"

Amanda said, "Competition is a veil that needs to be torn. Until you can see things in a different light, you have no option but to compete."

"Let's change the subject: If I'm not mistaken, you mentioned that humans had a rudimentary language when you arrived."

Amanda said dismissively, "They had names for some objects. That was the extent of it. They used language to signal to each other. A little more sophisticated than apes."

"And this account can be trusted because you have historical records, I take it. This is not speculation or anything like that, is it?

"That is right," said Amanda, shaking her head.

"I wish I was there to see exactly how advanced early humans were in language usage, " said David.

"This is clear to me: Had we not interfered, there would be no history, technology, or anything like that on Earth. If language was ever going to develop naturally to the level necessary for civilization, it would have taken hundreds of thousands of years. By that time, a natural disaster might have wiped out all traces of humans before they even started. A case in point is that we have already averted several extinction-level events in the past 50,000 years to preserve humans and allow them to mature. We did what we did mostly for selfish reasons, but we also enabled human civilization to come into existence."

David said, "One more question. What was the reason you chose me? I can speculate, but I want to hear it from you."

"For your work in recognizing the importance of stories and distinguishing between rudimentary language context vs. the advanced form. And the fact that it involved certain abilities, including suspension of reality. To us, that was a unique perspective. Recognizing that language for humans is not simply a tool for communication or signaling—it is a tool for creating and telling stories, which is at the core of progress."

David said, "Wow, I'm glad I finally found the reason."

The Exit Interview

For a few moments, there was an uneasy silence between them. Then David asked, "What have you learned from humans?"

Amanda said, "We have learned a lot. The most notable is music."

"You mean you had never heard music before?" David asked.

Amanda said, "Our biological ancestors played music. We had no need for it. We were never in a position to learn anything from our ancestors that did not have to do with survival and resolving the life-and-death situation we were facing. However, as we observed humans, we integrated music into our consciousness. We enjoy it. Do you remember the piano in the blue hall downstairs? Suddenly, I have the urge to play it. If you are done with breakfast, we can go downstairs and spend some time there. My time is solely dedicated to you today."

David followed Amanda to the blue room as Amanda referred to it, even though from what David could gather, the walls in every room in the house could dynamically change to any color. Hidden in the ceiling, the lights appeared to emit from underneath the round ceiling tiles. The light was diffused evenly and smoothly.

Amanda said, "Relax, enjoy yourself, and let me know what you want me to play."

Amanda sat on the bench at the grand piano. She caressed the piano keys, moving over all of them. Her white overalls contrasted the ebony finish of the 9-foot concert piano, and she said, "I love this instrument; it embodies the ingenuity of humans and is what can eventually help humanity to come out of the cycle of self-inflicted pain. In contrast to all the tools humans have made for destruction in the name of defense, this tool only creates pure joy. In our eyes, this has helped us maintain our positive outlook toward humans."

Amanda smiled and continued while staring at David, "What would you like me to play for you?"

David said, "Whatever is your favorite. It will give me a glimpse of what Gods like."

"I have many favorites. The piece I am going to play is for my human emotions," Amanda said. And she played a piece that David could not recognize. It was a sad piece and expressed a sense of loss and remorse.

***

When she was done, David noticed a drop of tear flowing down her cheek.

"David, would you like to take a walk with me on the beach?" Amanda asked.

"Yes, that's a great idea."

Amanda led the way. The sliding door of the room opened to a balcony. They walked onto a platform that appeared to be a lift; there were no walls. Moments later, they were on the beach.

David said, "So, what happens after this?"

Amanda paused for a moment and continued, "Now comes the hard part about our conversations. One piece of information missing from the manuscript I gave you is the last chapter of our conversation. We call this the Exit Interview. Out of billions of humans on earth, we have come to know a few; out of the few, we decided to have frank conversations with a smaller group. And you are among them. As I mentioned in the manuscript, the similarities between humans and our ancestors would also enhance our knowledge of our history. However, we did not want to overstep our prime directive, the non-interference in human lives. The best solution we came up with was to initiate this contact when the individual of interest was very close to the final moments of life. Our sensors can detect this with extreme accuracy. Our technology can dilate the perceived time for the individual in those final moments, which will allow for meaningful interaction. Now, ethically, we do not feel like we are deceiving them. We give them a choice to be in an interactive mode if they want, and if they so choose, we continue. If not, we end the interactive session, and the individual dies naturally within seconds, as expected. We cannot tell them the truth about the nature of the interaction and the last step until the end of the interview because otherwise, panic and the stress of death will overwhelm them. In your case, I told you that you could leave if you chose to, but then you would not have certain experiences by being with me. I hope you still feel you made the right choice."

"So, I take it that I'm very close to death then," David sighed. His voice was slightly shivering and lower than normal.

Amanda sounded sad, "I am afraid so."

David responded, "I could be angry and think you took advantage of me or were dishonest. But I am only sad and think this is not fair."

Amanda said, "Why do you think this is unfair? I thought you actually gained from this encounter."

"If I am going to die, what is the point of this interview? Don't you think that is very selfish of the collective?"

Amanda said, "I thought you were the type of person who wants an experience for the sake of that moment. Isn't that what matters the most? Besides, your participation will add to our knowledge base and be shared with our collective and, hopefully, at some point, even with humans. So, your views will live on. Isn't that also an important factor in human life? Is that not adequate for you? Life, especially in its biological form, by nature, is very fragile and limited in time and scope. I can assure you that your lifespan has not been affected at all by this encounter. Whether we met or not, you were to die of a massive heart attack."

David said, "My only objection is that I cannot share my experience with anybody else. My experience ends here, and there seems to be no point in this newly acquired knowledge. I would have been happy if I could use this experience even if I was aware of it only in my subconscious. Maybe if I had a chance to interact with others, even briefly, I would feel differently."

"So you find it a waste of time?"

"Maybe it is different for you, but sharing the experience is extremely important for us. I think you mentioned two aspects: one has to do with the immediate gratification of the experience, and the second is knowing that your experience has had an impact on the lives of others. But there is a third aspect: you need an opportunity to share your experience with others."

Amanda replied, "Let me be blunt. Is it sharing that is important or recognition by others? 'sharing' makes it sound so innocent. It is as if what you do is for others. But maybe recognition by others is the ultimate goal. You want to be recognized for what you have done. And the only problem with our encounter is that nobody else but yourself will ever know about it. Isn't that it?"

David sounded agitated, "What's wrong with that, even assuming that is the case? Is that too much to ask? If it is true that we are, in a sense, your children, then you should know us by now. We cannot live without meaning. *We* give meaning to life. How could life have any meaning if there is no recognition? This experience is making that clearer to me. It just takes different forms whether you are religious or an atheist. In the face of our mortality, recognition and knowing that we will somehow remain, at least in name, gives us permanence and meaning."

Amanda fired back, "But that is an unreasonable thing to ask. We have conquered death. But even we shut down voluntarily. And all collective members eventually choose to shut down and give way to fresh ideas."

"I am not asking for eternal life if that is what you understand from my complaint."

Amanda said, "Humans fear death because it is a total unknown. You have very limited time on earth. You don't control when you are born, and you don't control when you die. Humans strive to leave a mark because that is the only way they can feel immortal. They want to leave behind something that carries their name. One thing they cannot do is leave behind their consciousness. If your consciousness persisted, none of that would have mattered. Then, you could truly live and embrace the gift that is life to observe the universe. We have solved the issue by creating a continuum of consciousness for each collective member. A collective member's consciousness carries over to the next member. Some of the awareness is public and shared with everybody. Some are private, which only the member and their descendants know. And I think that humans simply have to wait until they achieve that. You have to accept that you have limited time, and you can observe what you can, and some of what you observe is for you only, and you cannot share it."

David now sounded confident, "I think there need to be exceptions. Don't take me wrong; I am honored that you selected me. But there is more to the story: from what I gathered from your writings, you intervened in the normal events on Earth by modifying the human DNA. And I was one of the first to suspect that there had been a sudden change. I have dedicated my whole life to this discovery. If you felt that the discovery made it worthwhile to have an interview with me, then I need to have enough time to experience the joy of discovering and sharing this find. The remembrance does not need to be conscious. And I do not need to remember anything about this encounter. Based on what I know from your technology, this is possible. For me, this makes my life complete. I could not have asked for anything more. And I think it is not too much to ask you. If I am representing humanity, I can confidently say that you have learned a lot from us. For the moment, granted, it has been mostly from our mistakes. But I hope we will soon be able to transcend the mistakes."

Amanda was silent for a few moments. She shook her head and closed her eyes.

Awakening

David found himself on a park bench. He felt like an old man. He thought, *Wow, I fell asleep; I'm too young for that.* There was a commotion—a lot of people. He stood up and looked around. He sensed a festive environment. He tried to remember how he got there. It was coming back to him. There was supposed to be a music festival featuring musicians from around the world. And even though he had lived many years in the area, and this was a frequent event, he had always missed previous festivals. Not this time, he had thought. This time, he'd planned ahead, appeared hours earlier to find a good spot, and sat on the bench looking at the ocean. Evidently, that was when he had fallen asleep.

The sun was setting now. He consoled himself that he deserved this time off since he was not used to taking any time off.

The music started. David stood up and joined others, uncharacteristically clapping and swaying with them. A woman approached. She looked familiar. But David could not pinpoint how and from where he knew her.

She said, "Hi, do you mind if I join you? I'm here to dance. My name is Amanda."

David looked at her and cocked his head sideways, as he always did when trying to remember, "You look very familiar. Today, I'm told, is the day of friendship and harmony. You chose a good day to look familiar." And he smiled as he was gazing into her eyes.

Amanda took David's hand and said, "I love music. Isn't it amazing?"

"It is, it truly is."

The End

About the Author

M. Nariman is an inventor and the founder of an engineering, automation, and robotics company. He has interests in philosophy, physics, robotics, and anthropogeny, the study of the origins of humanity.